Dante's Deal

Dante's Deal

By Aleka Nakis

Resplendence Publishing, LLC
http://www.resplendencepublishing.com

Resplendence Publishing, LLC
2665 N Atlantic Avenue, #349
Daytona Beach, FL 32118

Dante's Deal
Copyright © 2010, Aleka Nakis
Edited by Tiffany Mason
Cover art by CBK, www.creationsbykendra.com

Print format ISBN: 978-1-60735-298-3

Print release: June 2011

The Italian men of Quickie's Burgers and Wings in Hollywood are true heroes.
To Alessandro Cutrera and Fabrizzio De Carne
for indulging a terrible romantic and correcting my Italian.
Grazie!

Chapter One

"*We have a deal.*"

The four simple words were the sweetest of music to Dante Morelli's ears and made his pulse race. He glanced at the signed documents on the conference table and smiled. Nothing was more satisfying than a contract that placed power in the center of his palm. Power he could multiply to enhance his profit sheet.

"Good work," Dante replied, fisting his right hand to contain his excitement. As the leader of an international corporation, displaying casual emotion was the best option when in a meeting. "Have no doubt, gentlemen. This small venture will lead to much greater ones. Securing the—"

The office door slammed against the wall, and a whirlwind of fresh citrus and floral swirled through the room and filled his nose. The gorgeous and ultra-feminine apparition entered his conference room like a volcano spewing lava off a steep cliff and into the sea. The damn woman caused time to stop.

"*Mio Dio*, what an unexpected pleasure," Dante Morelli breathed, rubbing his fist over his accelerating heart rate.

Swallowing the knot sealing off his airway, Dante rose to his feet and yanked on his tie, making way for oxygen to reach his lungs.

Astoundingly, the bundle of female feistiness that stormed in on his meeting caused his hardened legal team to gawk and their mouths to drop. It was as if they witnessed the appearance of a ghost—a beautiful and captivating spirit. Studying their reactions, Dante laughed, approving of her influence.

Stupenda.

She is good.

Much to his discomfort, Dante had the urge to drape his jacket over Sapphy's shoulders, hide what she'd become, drag her home, and tuck her tempting body under the covers and away from the view of other men. Each click of her heels on the polished floor was a sharp tap on his chest, shooting desire and simultaneous guilt through every nerve of his being. His body reacted on an inappropriate and guttural level that was out his comfort zone.

He adjusted his jacket to conceal the physical evidence of his desire. No hard-ons allowed in the corporate boardroom. Especially, not from the Chief Executive Officer. Especially not when it came to someone as dear as the woman standing before him. She fueled a flame that should not burn and appeared to have no problem doing so. Actually, she looked like she enjoyed doing it.

"Dismiss the team, we have business to discuss," Sapphy demanded.

Pinching the bridge of his nose, Dante attempted to appear unaffected by her opulent appearance and unsuccessfully tried to ignore his physical arousal. Her skirt wrapped tight above her knees and accompanied a light blue jacket, hugging every inch of her gracious figure. When she placed her palms on the broad mahogany table and fixed him with that exquisite gaze of piercing sapphires, her breasts would have spilled into his hands if it weren't for the cream-colored camisole she wore.

Rich, ebony hair framed her olive-colored face and reflected the afternoon sun, streaming in from large office window. Not only had she had developed into a beauty, but there was an aura of confidence and authority radiating from her that didn't come easy to women her age.

"It is such a pleasure to see you. Please join us," he said, inviting her to sit in the empty chair to his left.

Not one of his executives had blinked since the moment she'd strolled into the room. She'd mesmerized them like she had the young men at the nightclub a dozen years ago. He grinned at Sapphy's innate ability to command everyone's attention without even asking for it.

"I'm sorry, Dante." Gabriella, his stepsister, scurried to his side and interrupted his thoughts. "I tried to tell her you were in a meeting, but she wouldn't wait. She barged past the reception and into your office without any explanation."

"I don't need an explanation to enter any office in this building. I am the 'S' of SD Holdings—the big neon letters sprawled across the rooftop." Sapphy threw Gabriella a challenging smile. "Now, Gabriella, are you here on a legitimate office task to document minutes of this meeting, or are you on the way to a fancy luncheon with the latest socialites in Naples?"

"Well, I—"

"Thank you, Gabriella. There is no need to explain." Dante cleared his throat. "We are family. Sapphyra belongs, and is always welcome, here."

Sapphy's eyes blazed with something more than annoyance, but it was the sternness of her face that burned straight to Dante's gut. Despite his outward calm, and regardless of how well he disguised his discomfort, he knew that trouble was close on their heels. She was annoyed and would not be easy to dismiss. What had caused the abrasive attitude in the typically agreeable girl he'd known?

Sapphy glanced at the tall man who had silently followed her into the room and nodded for him to take a seat. He looked familiar, but Dante couldn't place him. The protective pose of the other man's body behind Sapphy troubled Dante more than being unable to identify him.

"Truly a pleasure," Dante repeated, reaching for Sapphy and giving her a quick hug and kissing each of her cheeks. "I'm so happy you are visiting." He then turned to the silent man who had eyeglasses perched on the edge of his nose and extended his hand. "Dante Morelli."

"Pleased to meet you in person, Mr. Morelli," the stranger replied in an American accent. "Cosmo Papadopoulos."

Dante didn't miss the casual placement of Papadopoulos's left hand on Sapphy's back as he reached for Dante's hand.

"Mr. Papadopoulos may be new to some of you." Sapphy addressed the executives sitting around the conference table with a casual grace that belonged to a princess. "He joined the New York office last month and is a prized addition to our legal team across the Atlantic."

The group welcomed the newcomers and made room for the duo to join them at the table, but Sapphy remained standing, a hint of uneasiness apparent in the rigid line of her back.

"I have news to share with you, which I believe you will like a great deal," Dante said, hoping notice of the latest company transaction would appease her. After all, the proposition was like found money to SD. "There has been a handsome offer on the family land on Zantè. We were discussing how to expedite the sale."

Her pupils grew big, and he thought he saw her lower lip tremble. She didn't speak, but lines creased her beautiful forehead. She appeared to be standing on coals. Sapphy jumped when he touched her arm, and he pulled back his hand, burned by rejection.

"I don't." Shrugging out of reach, she dropped onto the large executive chair and placed her colorful briefcase on the table. "The land on *Zakynthos*, which is the proper name of the island, will remain in the family. I have no intention of parting with it."

Dio mio, she is fantastic.

Her shapely leg hung over her knee, and her intertwined fingers rested in a casual, yet powerful, manner on her slightly exposed thigh. She may have grown into a very beautiful woman, but her childhood spunk had not dissipated. His Sapphy spoke her mind and didn't hesitate to disagree with the majority. What a refreshing addition to his boardroom.

His gaze dropped back to her feet, featured in a pair of very sexy high heels that displayed the perfect shape of her seemingly endless legs. He imagined running his palm over her silky skin.

I should not be thinking of her legs or the fullness of her breasts. Sapphyra is the same Sapphy she has always been. No matter how she has grown.

She was his late father's best friend's only child. And most importantly, she was under Dante's protection and his responsibility for the time being. He kicked his libido back into a proper holding pattern.

"Why would you be opposed to making a hefty

sum on property you have not visited in years? It is just sitting there." He resumed his place at the head of the table and flattened his hand over the cool surface, lowering his voice to the proper and protective tone he reserved exclusively for her.

"Honestly, Sapphy, this transaction makes perfect sense."

"I haven't visited the estate because I've been an ocean away studying." She raised her hands to the side of her head and crooked her index and middle fingers to denote quotations. "Do you think I've had the opportunity to kick back and enjoy Zakynthos in any way?"

"Exactly why we should sell the place." He closed his fingers over hers and squeezed. "Sapphy, the offer on the Zantè property is a pleasant surprise. I have not thought of that specific piece of land in years, and to have Andreas Petos offering us above market value is much more than convenient for our plans. Forty point seven million Euros is a good day's work. We will review the details in a little while. Okay?"

"No need. We're not selling." Her tempting pink lips formed an adorable, stubborn pout.

"I do not understand," Dante said. "Is there something going on that you want to tell me about? Has something happened that I am not aware of?"

Sapphyra summoned her strength to maintain the façade of power and bravado, pulling her hand from under Dante's. Meeting him under these conditions was very unsettling. It put the urgency of her situation in perspective, and made her feel like a rabbit on a dog track. She found all of the etiquette and procedure required in the conference room forced and dry. The manner in which they spoke wasn't natural, and the communication was stiff. It was as if they were two puppets, controlled and maneuvered by the most unimaginative puppeteer on an impressive, yet impersonal, corporate stage.

Ridiculous, pompous Boardroom-Geppetto stole my life. Now, I have to act all proper to appear strong. So not so.

Blinking to shutter any emotion from her eyes, she looked away from Dante and accepted the stale predicament she was in. She lifted her chin in a much more confidant act than her stomach admitted to. Damn butterflies were having a field day down there, and she was grateful to have skipped lunch.

"Sapphyra?" Dante was staring at her as if she was from a different planet. Everyone in the room was staring.

The stifling air whittled away her poise, but the property was not up for discussion. Her father's instructions had been very specific: *The estate is Eleni's. When she finds you, sign it to her. Then tell her how much I love her.*

"Dante, the Zakynthos land is part of my childhood, and I will keep it for future use. I don't care what Petos has offered. It isn't for sale." She scraped her lower lip, wondering how many cards she should lay on the table. "I'd like to spend time vacationing there."

He nodded. "No problem. I will arrange for us to retain a parcel overlooking the sea. We will build a small villa for weekend jaunts. I am certain Petos will agree."

She tried to still her bobbing foot, but her nerves stretched beyond that possibility. She couldn't control it. Her leg moved even faster.

"Then it is settled," Dante continued, a grin

magically appearing on his handsome face. "You will be happy with the deal."

Damn, he was patronizing her. Dante was being thoughtful, considerate, and typical Dante. He appeared sincere, but her belly twisted as his gaze held hers. Even though Dante had never openly denied her a single thing, his cajoling manner needed to disappear. She was no longer a child.

Sapphyra sighed and shut her eyes for a brief moment. She was the business partner he'd managed to keep quiet and satisfied. She was a duty he had to attend to and a temporary inconvenience in his life. Well, not for long.

"A house? On a small parcel?"

Dante bent his head in confirmation, his dark hair moving like liquid waves over his forehead as he looked past her. "Gabriella, please arrange a short call to Petos and explain that there will be an addendum to the deal."

Sapphy pressed her hand against her abdomen. The sensual drawl of the other woman's name off Dante's lips made her nauseous. He pronounced every letter with a soft roll, starting deep in his throat and letting it linger on his tongue. But, when it came to her name, it was short and direct: Sa-fee.

Dante Morelli, the feared and respected powerhouse, was very comfortable in this magnificent and masculine boardroom. He shined with supremacy. His physical strength matched his mental dedication, and the tall, broad shouldered, Italian managed to achieve any objective he set his mind to with an unnatural ease. His stellar reputation and honest business practices only added to the industry's faith in his abilities.

She, on the other hand, found it hard to assimilate

to this environment. Surrounded by the stark and competent associates, the Spartan furnishings, and the cold marble floor, Sapphy felt empty and lost. How was she supposed to compete?

"If Petos has a problem, I'll discuss the change with him myself," Dante instructed. "Let me know if you need anything."

"Yes, Dante." Gabriella rose from her chair and smoothed her Gucci skirt over her shapely hips. "I will take care of it."

"*Grazie, ciccia.*" Dante's eyes filled with appreciation, and a pang of envy pierced through Sapphy as the term of endearment reached her ears. He then turned to the legal team. "Gentlemen, you have your assignment. Now, if you will excuse us." He leaned back in his chair. "I need to discuss matters with my wife."

A collective breath escaped the other men as they gathered their papers and jumped from their seats.

"Nice to see you again... *Signora* Morelli." Antonio Cazebri, a renowned international attorney, gave a slight bow and backed away from the table, tripping over his heels. "Dante," he added, turning to leave with the staff.

"Have a good afternoon, Antonio," Sapphyra said in a pleasant voice. "Don't forget to leave my estate on Zakynthos intact."

The lawyer stopped mid-stride and glanced back at Dante. Like an ice statue on a buffet table with lights beating on him, beads of perspiration collected on his forehead.

For once, Dante looked at her. Really looked at her.

She casually bent her head to the side and reiterated, "I told you: I've no intention of selling the land. It will remain in the family."

"Sapphy, you have never questioned my judgment before. This is a very straightforward opportunity that makes all the sense in the world. You need to trust me."

"It has nothing to do with your judgment, Dante." She pulled her case off the table and onto her lap. "However, I do not wish to part with the property, and you have no right to make that decision."

"I have every right." His forehead creased and he stood, commanding everyone's attention. From the breadth of his shoulders, to the broadness of his chest beneath his crisp white shirt, to the intensity of his large, olive shaped eyes, Dante presented the ideal picture of a mythological god about to seduce his subjects into acting on his behalf. "I have been making these decisions for years, and *this* decision has been made."

"Not if I disagree." Sapphyra clasped her new Kelly bag to prevent her fingers from twisting aimlessly.

Step-sis-in-law coughed and sashayed across the room on two thousand dollar heels to Antonio. "Why don't you wait for me to contact you?" Gabriella suggested, throwing an elegant, yet tactless, knowing glance toward the attorney. "I am sure Mr. Morelli will have further instructions for you in a short while." Fiddling with her designer collar, Gabriella's long, thin fingers played across her giraffe-like neck.

"There is no need." Dante's terse voice left no room for rebuttal. His gaze singed Sapphy's self-assurance, but she wasn't about to back down. She couldn't.

"Yes, there is. We have other things to consider," she added.

She glanced at Cosmo, her much needed friend,

and raised her eyes to the ceiling. *Don't talk. Not yet.*

Cosmo was supposed to make her look official and use his legal expertise to back her when necessary, but at this point, the conversation was between her and Dante. She had it. Sapphy needed to exert her authority and gain control.

"We absolutely must discuss a few things," Dante agreed. "Your obligation is to your studies, and my obligation is to this company. I will not allow anyone to question me or my commitment, and particularly not in the manner you have chosen today." He stood and stretched before leaning forward to secure his large hands on the mahogany surface, daring her to object.

"My obligations to my studies ended last semester. I now have two lovely degrees sitting in my center drawer waiting to be framed."

"Ended?" Dante's shock reverberated through every cell in Sapphy's body.

"Yes."

"I thought you wanted to pursue your PhD."

"No. I'm not interested in a PhD. *You* wanted me to do that," she said, rolling her eyes. "What difference does it make, Dante? I'm here, and I won't let you sell the land."

"It makes a big difference." Done with the charade, Dante was not letting anything go. "If you have a sincere concern with a decision I have made, you are well aware of how we could discuss any dispute. Bombarding a meeting with attitude is not the proper way to conduct business."

Here was the condescending and arrogant Dante she knew. Talking down to her and treating her like a two year old. Well, she wasn't a child any longer. She had an opinion and a choice and would be heard.

She'd considered telling him about her father's request. She'd actually planned on it because she knew in her heart that he would honor it. But after that little display of Mr. Control Freak, she'd get it done on her own.

"Dante—" Gabriella's sweetest voice attempted to mask the tension in the room.

"Enough. Thank you, Gabriella." He didn't bother to turn and address his stepsister. Focused exclusively on Sapphy, he scrutinized every move she made as she attempted to sit calmly in her chair. "Antonio has his instructions and knows what to do. It is time for the three of you to leave. Sapphyra and I have things to discuss." Dante glared directly at Cosmo, sitting silently beside her.

"In private," he snarled.

Cosmo stood and followed the exodus of the remaining employees from the conference room. The door latched behind her support system and the hollow pit in her core grew.

"There is no need for rudeness." Sapphy bobbed her foot, intentionally this time, and gave Dante what she hoped was a nonchalant smile. "Cosmo is my financial and legal advisor, as well as one of my best friends. This may be news to you, but our so-called marriage isn't a buried secret from *my* friends."

"Our *marriage* isn't a secret. Period."

Muscles corded down the side of his neck and the hollow at the base of his throat pulsed. His chest rose as he took a breath and then exhaled loudly. Clearly, he wasn't happy with her surprise visit any longer.

"True, the circumstances of our wedding imposed atypical stress on each of us. But, we have made it work to our benefit. You have been able to study hard." Once again, he pinched the bridge of his nose. "By committing our efforts to SD Holdings, we've tripled our joint income."

He omitted the fact that the efforts to their business were all his. She'd barely contributed over the past five years. Spending a few weeks in the summer helping in the office didn't add up to much. She'd let him shoulder all the responsibility and now, the remorse of her actions unsettled her.

"The restructuring gamble has paid off, and SD Holdings is climbing the international ladder of prestige," he continued, pacing the floor. "However, you seem to have forgotten that you are undermining our union's purpose by publicly disagreeing with me. We must always present ourselves as a unified front."

"Oh, come on, Dante. That's so medieval." She opened the folio and searched through sheets of paper. "I may be younger than you, but I'm not an idiot. I have every right to an opinion, and I don't appreciate you talking down to me."

"Then don't give me reason to."

Talk about patronizing!

Ceasing his pacing, he rested on the edge of the table and stretched long legs in front of him. "I never said or thought that you are an idiot," he added in a low voice, crossing his arms over his chest and staring at the floor. "Since you have abandoned your schooling, what have you been doing in America while I thought you were studying?"

"I haven't abandoned anything. I completed my formal education last month, and I have been following the daily operations of SD Holdings without interfering. Learning how this company operates from afar has not been easy, but it has been gratifying." She paused, searching his eyes for a reaction. He wore a mask, a mask of irritation and let nothing else through.

"The time has come for me to take an active role in the enterprise our fathers have left us."

"The time has come?"

"Yes." She lengthened her back to appear tall and confident. "In monitoring the company's activities, I've agreed with your methods."

"Nice to know," he jabbed.

"However, I don't see any need to sell the property on Zakynthos, and I must disagree with your decision if you insist on executing it." She met his gaze and refused to look away. "As for your question, yes, Dante, the time has come for me to alleviate you from the sole responsibility you've been bearing for the company. I'm here, and I'm ready to work." Sapphy let out a long breath. Acting official drained her energy and creativity like leaving the headlights of a parked car on overnight.

He cleared his throat and pushed away from the table. As he walked over to the large window, she focused on his broad back, admiring not only his physique, but his strength. The emotions of annoyance and stubbornness fighting with the admiration and gratefulness she felt toward him made it difficult to maintain her role of a shrew in boardroom.

"That is good, Sapphy." His fingers messed through his hair, and then he switched to speaking in his native tongue. "However, it isn't necessary for you to do anything from afar. You should be working here, and we will work together to assimilate you into headquarters. Slowly." He turned and faced her. "However, I am not pleased with the way you have approached the issue. There was no need for a public tirade or for you to storm—"

"Whether you are pleased with my conduct has nothing to do with the fact that we're partners in this venture. I have just as much of a right as you do to be heard and considered."

It was difficult to appear cold as ice when her insides smoldered. Her conscience was like the sticky stuff left in the fondue pot after the second bottle of wine had been emptied. But, once again, she had no choice. Letting things out and asking for his help and guidance was a sign of weakness. She had to maintain a tough persona—no matter how forced the role felt.

A muscle in the center of his cheek twitched and his jaw squared. His shoulders stood stiff and he stuffed his hands in his pants pockets.

"You are always considered," Dante said in a low voice.

Sapphy pretended not to hear and pulled a manila folder from her case. "On page nineteen, paragraph three of our marital contract, it states that when I do not agree with a decision made for SD, it shall be stalled for a month of investigation and will require both of our approvals for any further action to be taken." She snapped the folder shut. "I will not agree for you to sell the property in any timeframe."

His lips formed a stringent line and his gaze filled with disbelief. She'd never questioned him in the past, but he needed to know that she was a grown woman who knew her mind and heart. And that was the main message she wanted to get across at the moment. She was not the girl he had married five years ago in the hospital chapel. Nor was she the girl he'd put on a plane to New York only a few months earlier. That girl had morphed into a competent and professional woman. Hopefully, one that could hold her ground in the circle he lived in.

"We started off on the wrong foot today." Dante cleared his throat. "Let us take a step back and begin over." He opened his arms and offered her a hug. "Welcome home, *dolcezza*."

She remained seated and glared at his outstretched hands. *Not this time. You will not win me over with a touch.*

Pushing her body against the chair, she gazed around the room, searching for physical strength to continue. Her insides rattled, but on the surface, she didn't break a sweat. She placed her personal feelings aside and focused on protecting their company while securing her role in SD Holdings.

"I'd prefer it if we move to my office." Dante dropped his arms to his side. "We will be more comfortable. *Daccordo*?"

Inhaling deeply, she rose and steadied her legs. Clutching her briefcase, she followed him. How silly for a bag to give her so much confidence. But it did. And it was worth every dollar she'd paid for the Kelly exclusive and worth the effort and extra time needed for the special order.

Leading her to the far end of the room, Dante held the door to his private office for her to enter. Surprisingly, he locked it behind him, making it clear they were not to be disturbed. He walked to the desk and invited her to take a seat. Defying his suggestion, she removed a copy of the page she'd referred to earlier from the file, and careful not to touch him, slid the document across the desk.

"The contract is in black and white. The land on Zakynthos will not be sold." She closed the dossier, held it against her chest and crossed her arms over the smooth leather.

Sometimes, things happened for a reason, and this was certainly one of those times. It was a good thing she'd studied the contract on the flight over. She hadn't expected Petos to try to take her only connection to her family away from her, but at least she had an ironclad way to protect herself and didn't need to rely on Dante.

"I have arrangements to make," she said. "I'll let you go for now, and we'll touch base later. You can reach me at the *Grand Hotel Vesuvius* if you need me before Monday morning."

Dante quickly circled the furniture and came to stand in front of her. Firmly, yet gently, he wrapped his fingers around her upper arms and insisted on her attention.

"Since when do you stay at a hotel when you come home?"

"Dante, we need to stop this pretense when we're alone." She scraped her teeth over her bottom lip. "We're not a happily married couple that runs into each other's arms when we meet. Let's keep things proper and professional, as you say—"

"You are not happy?"

She'd thought he'd be jumping for joy to be released from his obligations to her. Rather, he acted as if he wanted to maintain the status quo.

"Let me rephrase that." She met his gaze, hoping he'd move a little further away from her. It was hard to breathe with him so physically close. "I've come to Naples so that we can discuss the terms of the divorce and the future of our company. We can't avoid the issue any longer. I turn twenty-three in two months, and I must deal with this as a mature and professional adult."

"No problem. We'll have dinner, alone, tonight, to discuss the company and our relationship properly."

"Not tonight." She shook her head. By insisting they discuss matters, he was making things so difficult.

"We can't pretend that we have more than we do between us, or that we don't have lives to get on with."

Sapphy had strolled into SD headquarters with the intention of showing Dante that she was a competent professional and able to look after herself. She had been ready to give him his walking papers and cut him loose. Now, after spending less than an hour with him, she didn't know what she wanted. So, there was no question that she needed her own space.

"I will stay in Naples this weekend. It's not appropriate to bring Cosmo to Sant'Anna," she said, moving her hand out of his reach and waiting for a response.

A dark shadow spread over his face. Dante was having a very difficult time about not getting his way. But, that was something he'd need to get used to. She had to do things on her own from now on. She wouldn't pass the decision making to him.

"Will he be staying long?"

"No. He has personal things to deal with back home." She tucked a tendril of hair behind her ear and shifted her weight. "Cosmo flies back to New York on Monday and will not return for two weeks. We have much work to review before then."

"Work on the weekend?" Dante raised a dark brow and smirked, as if calling her bluff. He cleared his throat. "Even though our marriage was arranged and is on paper only, I have never flaunted any disrespect or dishonor of our vows for foreign eyes to devour. I expect no less from you."

He's worried that I'll ruin his reputation if I'm seen with a different man. An added benefit I didn't foresee. I really do have much to learn. I didn't even consider the scenario.

"Dante, now that we'll be living in the same city,

you need to heed your own words. No double standard." Since he brought it up, Sapphyra was going to take full advantage of the point. "I have no desire of airing dirty laundry for the tabloids."

"I've never paraded around in public with any other woman on my arm." He switched to Italian. He did that often when he didn't censor his words. "Not once have I been indiscreet about our personal life."

Unable to identify or label the emotion that flared in his eyes, she looked away and gazed out the window, considering his words. He had never bothered to parade *her* around on his arm. Did the public even realize they were married?

"No, you haven't," she whispered. "Our marriage is different and absolutely not conventional. I'm not a fool, and I didn't expect you to remain celibate for all these years because we had a legal union on paper." A younger Sapphy may have dreamed of such devotion, but today, she was too realistic to believe such a thing.

"We had this discussion long ago," Dante reminded her. "On our wedding day to be exact. We agreed to live our personal lives as if we were single. However, our chief concern, then and now, was and is for this marriage to appear genuine to the business community. You know the arrangement."

"I do." Heat crept over her body at the thought of a true and complete relationship with him.

Not once had she seen him pictured with a woman, not once had she learned of him being with another woman, but not once had she believed that a man like him could go without sex for any amount of time.

"We'll be living in the same city, we need to make it look even more real between us," she continued. "We can't afford to appear...fake."

"*Sì*. No need to rehash the same things over and over."

She stood, and he reached for her. Kissing each of her cheeks in the same chaste greeting he'd offered since she could remember, he rested his hands on her shoulders.

"Under any circumstances and in any setting, it is good to see you, Sapphy. Welcome home."

"Thank you." Shivers travelled down her spine as his arms wrapped around her and pulled her against his chest. She closed her eyes and took a deep breath, inhaling the fresh and masculine scent so distinctly Dante.

Pulling out of his embrace, she gave him another big smile and headed toward the exit. She could do this. She could play in the big leagues with the best of them.

Chapter Two

"Ready," she announced, strolling through the reception area to where Cosmo waited and feathering her hand over her friend's shoulder. Even though she refused to look back, she could feel Dante's gaze follow her till she turned the corner.

Taking the elevator to the lobby in silence, Sapphy's stomach twisted and turned as if she were on a roller coaster ride. The moisture collecting on her nape was a testament to how so-not-suave and so-not-sophisticated she truly was, and the heat tingeing her cheeks made her feel like a circus clown.

"Hey, you all right?" Cosmo asked, nudging against her as they stepped off the lift.

"Not here," she warned, glancing about the elaborate lobby and hastening her stride. "There are cameras everywhere."

"In that case..." Cosmo placed his hand in the small of her back and leaned down, planting a kiss on her cheek and chuckling against her ear.

Ignoring him, she gathered her Kelly closer and gave the attendant a courteous nod as he bowed and opened on the large glass door.

"Mrs. Morelli," he said, showing her to the right.

"Your car is waiting."

The driver moved quickly to open the limo door, and Sapphy practically jumped into the vehicle. She needed to collect herself. Her nerves were shaken, and soon, her true state of being would be evident for all to see. She collapsed on the back seat.

I can't do this. What if he doesn't care and I look like a fool? What if he laughs at the bambolina?

But, and this but was what made it so difficult, Dante had never laughed at her before. He'd been a solid pillar of support since her father had passed away. Seventeen and alone, she'd depended on Dante and accepted his help. Originally, she'd tried to object, tried to convince her father that she was strong enough to make it on her own. She remembered every moment of that day. The uncertainty, the pain, and the surrender that had found comfort in a young and determined man, who put his life on hold for her.

"It's not right. Don't make me marry him," she had pleaded, scraping the vanilla flavored gloss off her lips until they pulsed with pain.

"Agape mou, it is for the best," her father had breathed, running thick, but frail, fingers down her arm.

"I'm capable of handling our affairs," she'd insisted, forcing the tears to stay hidden behind her eyes. "There is no reason for such extreme measures." She'd bent, and with shaky hands, had placed new slippers on her father's feet.

"I'm sorry, but the doctor will not allow me to leave. It has to be like this, my child." Struggling to inhale, her father had remained seated on the bed while she'd combed his hair.

Helping him stand, Sapphy had secured his robe over his green gown and had pulled the IV pole beside him. So as not to add to his stress, she'd smiled, raising her shoulders and shaking her head. "The location is not important."

"I will go to Italy and complete my degree while I work in our company. I will be smart and alert, and I won't allow others to exploit my position." She'd spoken in a low voice and had avoided meeting his gaze, attempting to hide the turmoil she'd felt. "I will not love any man. I will not fall prey to a gold seeking scoundrel."

"You are seventeen and beautiful, kori mou. You will not recognize the scoundrels. You are simply too young for that kind of insight." Andreas Poulos had kissed her twice on each cheek and then on the tip of her nose, just as he had since she was barely able to walk. He'd lowered the white lace over her face and had clasped her hand in his.

"Please." Tugging on his hand, she'd looked into her father's brilliant blue eyes, and begged for mercy, begged for him to reconsider his plan. "I won't be taken for a fool."

With tears in his eyes, her father had rejected her plea.

"He doesn't love me," she'd whispered.

"He will learn," Andreas had insisted. "Sapphyra, agape mou, this is truly the best for you. For one final time, you must trust me." It had been the tears streaking his cheeks that had urged her to accept the circumstances and had chipped at her resistance to the deal he'd secured with the Morellis.

"We have no living blood relatives to look after you when I am gone. At least, none that we know of. I believe that since God is kind, and since He chose to bless me with a daughter like you in my later years, He will unite you with my baby sister. And, when He does, you know what you must do. Until that time, Dante is your family."

Five years of Dante being her family had passed, and it wasn't fair to saddle him with a wife he loved as a sister.

"So, that went well," Cosmo said.

"Well?" Sapphy exclaimed, shaking her head to clear the memories of her wedding day. A day full of necessity and obligation. Not a day of white frills and balloons, nor laughter and romantic love.

"You're hallucinating." She bit the inside of her cheek and wondered why her friend was acting the way he was. What had Cosmo seen that she'd missed? "What was that kissy-feely display of affection in the lobby for?" Sapphy asked, smacking his knee.

"To worry your husband."

"He already is worried."

"I know," he said, giving her a smug smile. "You had him hot under the collar when he saw you. Good job, Sapphy."

"That wasn't my intention. I don't want a full-fledged war. I want him to recognize me for what I am. To hear me when I speak."

Her friend laughed. "By the looks of things in that conference room, Morelli will listen to what you have to say. You more than have his attention."

Capturing Dante's attention had never been the problem. She swallowed hard. "All I need to do is keep it," she mumbled, scooting forward in her seat and instructing the driver to take them to the hotel.

"What? We're not going for lunch down by the waterfront? No indulging ourselves in a lazy meal at *Gusto and Gusto*?"

"Sorry, babe. I know you're in awe of those funky orange aprons the waiters wear down there, but we don't have time for lingering in an elegant black and white film locale." She removed a gold band from her wallet and slid it on her finger. "Plus, I'm a married woman who can't be seen out in public with a handsome man I adore when I'm not with my husband."

"So, things changed?"

She nodded.

A pleased expression spread over her friend's face only to be replaced by a horrified grimace as the limo lurched to the right and passed two young women on a Vespa.

"Shit. They drive worse over here than they do in Manhattan." Grasping the door handle, he turned a ghastly pale color. A loud honk sounded. "Almost as bad as they drive in Athens."

Sapphy laughed and the tension of the morning dissipated a bit as she remembered her hometown.

"Aw, come on. You're in Italy. Relax." Now that she was away from the stifling conference room, she could be herself and not worry about her image. She smiled as the car rounded a fountain and pointed to a young man playing the accordion. "Enjoy."

"I'm not telling you not to *enjoy* yourself, Sapphy." Cosmo stared at her for a moment then took her hand in both of his. "Simply don't let the hustle and bustle of this place sweep you away and cause you to lose focus of your goal. Don't back down, and don't count on the first battle to win you the war."

"I'm not." She knew the drama hadn't even begun. Dante never took kindly to anyone questioning him, and he always accepted a challenge. "Just enjoy the buzz of Napoli while you can. You're not going to be here long enough to savor the true flavor of the city."

Cosmo smiled, but didn't relax as she suggested. His white fingertips contrasted greatly against the dark door handle as he gazed out at the congested street.

"Did you know Petos was interested in your father's property?" he asked.

"No," she replied. "I knew SD was trying to buy land he'd invested in so that we could manufacture security systems which the Union is looking to install at all major gateways, but nothing else. I hadn't expected to hear his name again so soon."

"I'm not making the connection." Cosmo huffed and grunted in the weird way he did when he was trying to understand. "Tell me about the time you met him in the Student Union again?"

"It wasn't much," she said, rolling her shoulders. "He came up to my table and introduced himself as a fellow Greek. He seemed nice enough. We talked about how it was to grow up in the suburbs of Athens and our summer vacations on the Islands."

"That's it?"

"That's it. I didn't even know his full name until a friend pointed it out after he'd left." She saw the next question in Cosmo's eyes and decided to answer it before he asked. "He introduced himself as Andy. No big production or anything special."

"You must be very careful," Cosmo said, squeezing her hand. "Once I return to New York, you will need to keep abreast of every development on your own."

"I know. I will." She pulled her hair back and tied it in a loose knot at her nape. "Why are you talking like I'm on my own? You're on the payroll. And, I'm entitled to counsel of my choice. That won't change."

"First, once the connection is concrete between you and your position at SD, people will try to take advantage of your lack of experience."

"Flashback," she cautioned, opening and closing her hands repeatedly. "You're sounding like my father."

He shrugged. "Second, Morelli will shelter you all

he can. I don't think he'll grant me access as he did before. It has now become personal."

"Nonsense." Sapphy waved a dismissive hand in the air. "If nothing else, Dante is fair. He wouldn't be petty when it comes to you. He's a professional."

"Mark my words, Mrs. Sapphyra Morelli. Prepare yourself."

Okay, so maybe she wasn't a powerhouse in the boardroom yet, but she wasn't a wilting lily either. She was smart, and she had inherited her father's genes. She'd absolutely grow into a force to be reckoned with. And, she'd do it her way.

* * * *

Dante rubbed the back of his neck and pushed away from his desk. He couldn't do a drop of work. He'd turned the computer on and off four times. He'd tried to place calls to the New York office, but found no one there since it was barely dawn oversees. He'd even attempted to review employee files, but stopped because he didn't feel it was fair in his state of mind. Finally, he'd given up and stared at the little sailboats on his computer screen.

Sapphy wanted out. She'd stated that she wanted to get on with life. A life without him.

So, what the hell did he waste his energy on all these years? He wasn't going to let her walk away without even trying to win her over? In the least, he deserved—no, he wanted—her full attention.

Frustration and a peculiar unease pulsed through his veins as he reviewed the day's events. Something wasn't right. He sensed it, and the tension lodged between his shoulder blades confirmed it.

Reading every word of their marriage contract twice, he'd found nothing that should have alarmed her and caused her to act the way she had. Even the clause she'd quoted earlier was insignificant. Sapphy knew that if she didn't want him to sell the property, all she had to do was ask...properly. Money was not an issue for them.

So what was it that had his Sapphy walking on coals? Most importantly, why was she hiding it from him? Had she found a different man? Was she in such a rush to divorce him in order to be with her lover?

Tension pounded against his temples. No other man would benefit from his sacrifice and diligence. She was his wife, and he'd insist she'd act accordingly. At least for the next two months.

He gazed out of the large window and watched people at the piazza relaxing beneath the orange umbrellas dotting the pavement. There were friends, gathering at a local café to drink their coffees, talk, and laugh the afternoon away. Dante didn't have time for such luxury. He had responsibilities to his company, his employees and their families, and to his wife.

The need to uphold his honor versed the urge to listen to his desires and tore at his peace of mind. What he wanted and what he should do were at different ends of the spectrum. Heaven help him. He'd always done the proper thing, and now, he wasn't certain if he could do the same.

Blowing out a long breath, he acknowledged that he would make time this weekend and learn what had upset Sapphy and caused her to act in such an aggressive manner. Her security and comfort were large parts of his responsibilities, and if he was honest with himself, they were his priorities.

The intercom buzzed, and Dante returned to the desk and hit the response button. Instructing the security guard to allow Antonio to visit, he didn't expect the instantaneous knock on his door.

"Why are you back at this time of the evening, and why are lurking outside my office with such restless anticipation?" Dante asked his best friend.

"The Petos deal," Antonio replied, in Italian. "Andreas refuses to continue with negotiations on the Naples factory if we pull away from the Zantè transaction."

"That's ludicrous." Dante sat and gestured for Antonio to do the same. "One has nothing to do with the other. We have agreed on the purchase terms for the factory. Besides, Zantè was not even mentioned until this morning. What does he want with Sapphy's property?"

"Personal. I think." Antonio raised his hand in exasperation. "There is no sound business reason."

"*Daccordo*," Dante replied, shaking his head. "Why Sapphy's property?"

"I'm not sure." Antonio set a file on the desk between them and shook his head, clearly as bewildered as his Dante. "What I do know is that Petos is bull-headed and won't budge."

"Seems like this might be an ethnic trait," Dante said, acknowledging Sapphy's Greek heritage. "She won't tell even me why she is acting the way she is."

Nodding, Antonio chuckled. "Believe me when I say I tried everything to reason with him. I even mentioned the property in your portfolio on Capri as an exchange," he paused, tapping his fingers on the manila folder. "Nothing."

Blood surged through Dante's veins and pounded in his head. Every muscle in his body tensed. He didn't lose, and especially not over something like this. There had to be more to the story; a missing link to the puzzle that he wasn't aware of.

"What are our options?" Dante asked.

A hiss slid from between Antonio's teeth. "Not many, Dante. Sell the Greek land and continue with things as planned before Sapphyra objected, or find a suitable alternative for the expansion property requested to seal the ECL deal."

"Elaborate on the latter."

"You are aware of the effort and time it took to find Petos's property. The old radio factory was the only one within city limits that could be converted and used for our purposes. The company searched for two months and exhausted all the possibilities before locating that run-down excuse of an opportunity." Antonio shifted in his seat and looked Dante in the eyes, waiting for a response.

"I know the history. That is not what I asked." Dante had led the team personally to bring this transaction into fruition. The welfare of many local people depended on whether he managed to make jobs available to them. He knew that a minimum of three hundred positions would be created if SD succeeded in gaining the contract. "What are our options at *this* point?"

"Find a new location for expansion, or talk with your wife," Antonio replied. "Sapphy has always been reasonable, and she can understand the benefits of this agreement. Just explain all the facts to her."

Flipping a pencil between his fingers, Dante mulled over the details. "In reality, Sapphy's property should not be part of the equation."

"We're not aware of all the facts. Do you know something I don't?" Antonio asked.

Dante shook his head. How the hell was he supposed to know what Sapphy was keeping from him?

"I put a team together to start a new search for more property." Collecting the file, Antonio looked away.

"I don't know why Sapphy is set on not selling." He tossed the pencil on the desk, and then picked up the same pencil to twirl. "Don't think I don't trust you or that I'm holding back any information, *amico mio*. I simply don't have the answer."

Nodding, Dante's best friend assumed his legal persona.

"We'll find an alternative. You'll figure out the answer to this riddle. And remember, there can be no secrets, and everything needs to be on the table and apparent to both parties when we execute the details of the divorce."

The pencil snapped in Dante's closed fist. He tossed it across the office.

"I'll talk to Sapphy."

* * * *

Dante wasn't accustomed to chasing Sapphy to speak with her, but he detoured into the car park of the *Vesuvius* on his way home. Ten after eleven. With the jet lag, she should still be awake. He made his way up to her suite and knocked on the door. Fisting his hands in his pocket, he prepared to lay one on Cosmo if he answered the door inappropriately.

Sapphy opened the door, wide eyed and surprised. A movie starring Raoul Bova played in the sitting area, a bowl of popcorn perched on the coffee table, and a throw was strewn over the couch.

"*Scusa Ma Ti Chiamo Amore?*" he asked, indicating the television set.

"Yes," she confirmed. "So much buzz, and I missed it while I was at school. Never had a chance to see it when I visited."

Leaning his head on the doorframe, he crossed his feet and nodded. Each time she came home, it was for an obligation that required all her attention. They rarely had time to relax and enjoy something as simple as a movie. It wasn't because he hadn't cared. He had. It just wasn't an option.

"Everything I have done for the past five years has been with you in mind. You have been a big part of me since the day you were born, and I have always loved and cared for you," Dante blurted before she had an opportunity to say anything. "We have a lifetime between us, Sapphy."

"Dante?" She rubbed her arms and stood aside, inviting him to enter. "What brought this on?"

"I do not like the way we left things in the afternoon. I do not like that you are staying in this hotel when you should be at Sant'Anna." His shoulder brushed against hers and he hesitated before walking on. He stood before her, longing to make it clear that he wanted her with him, but fearing he'd scare her away. "I never intended to distance you from your home. Did I make you feel not welcome?"

Rubbing his shoulders, he searched her eyes for an answer. Taking a step back, she shut the door and placed her palms on the hard surface behind her.

"No," she replied, shaking her head. "You've been better than a brother to me, and you've sacrificed more that I could ever have expected. I did not mean to sound ungrateful. I am," she breathed as a tear escaped her eye.

Cupping her trembling chin, he swept his thumb over the moisture trailing down her cheek and brushed it away. He studied her face, but didn't speak.

He recalled the tears she'd shed as she stood at the hospital chapel's entry on their wedding day. Standing amongst the Byzantine style icons laden with jeweled offerings for good health, which had adorned the tiny room, he had been awestruck when she'd appeared with a single pink rose in her hands. Thin candles had burned in the circular brass stands, adding the only light not entering from the stain-glassed windows and reflecting the moisture in her eyes. From the altar, Father Ignatius had smiled and invited for her to come before him.

Sapphy's feet had remained cemented to the arched entrance, giving the appearance that the heavy incense, swirling around the room, was holding her there.

Recognizing the distress on her beautiful face, he had gone to her and brushed the tears off her cheek. Taking her tiny hand in his, he had made her a promise to never let her down.

Five years later, this moment was too reminiscent. Too familiar.

"You've looked out for me, enabled me to finish my education, took care of our company, and have not ever complained or been disgruntled about it." She scraped her teeth over her bottom lip, pushing past him and sitting on a corner of the couch. "I will always appreciate what you've done, and I will always appreciate you."

"I chose to do that. You do not need to make it sound like a sacrifice of sorts." He claimed the chair nearest to her, moved the plush red pillows to the floor, and rested his elbows on his knees. "There is no reason for you to feel upset, and I certainly do not want you to cry. Do not concern yourself with small technicalities like the time limits in our marital contract." He never had a worry about the documents. The only thing he'd been concerned about was that she didn't feel ensnared by their marriage and trapped with him.

"Dante, my birthday is almost here. In two months, we will divorce. We need to face it." Wiping her cheeks, she looked away. Her pajama-clad leg bobbed nervously, and she no longer had the appearance of the business shark from the meeting room. This was his Sapphy—only grown up.

"*Bambolina,* look at me." He grinned as he captured her gaze and reached across the small space to stroke her cheek in a reassuring gesture. "The contract simply states that we are required to remain married for two more months. Nothing forces us to do anything we're not ready for. We can change the timing for the divorce and make it fit our own schedules. We'll work out the details between us. I will never let you down."

Sapphy's self-control crumbled a tiny piece at a time as the reality of her situation hit. Yearning to hide her face against his chest and sob, she grieved the end of her life as she knew it. The love she had for him was slotted to disappear one day soon. Regardless of when that day would be, she couldn't think of being without him, but she knew she had to let him go. It wasn't fair to him, no matter how much of her heart he'd be taking with him.

The past few months rushed back at her and the uneasiness returned. Considering the divorce had caused her to lie awake for endless nights. She'd cleaned her apartment within an inch of scrubbing the finish off her wood floors and taking the paint off the walls. Putting order in her home did little to reassure her that she could put the rest of her life in order.

Sapphyra, not Sapphy, had to emerge and learn how to fend for herself. She couldn't hold onto something she never really had in the first place.

"Sapphy?" Dante's voice seeped through her thoughts. "There is no need for haste. We can act as we please. Nothing will push our hand."

Things couldn't continue the way they were. She didn't want to live the lie of a fairy tale. Why prolong the inevitable?

"Thank you." Sapphy looked up at his handsome face. She wanted to stroke the dark stubble on his jaw, to soothe the tension from his forehead, but she didn't. She only smiled.

"I don't think I've told you how much I appreciate all you've done, but, thank you." Her chest was heavy, her eyes stung, but she couldn't pretend any longer to have tough skin when it came to Dante. "I've never doubted your intentions or your dedication, and you've done so much more than I think our fathers had ever anticipated."

"I would do it all again if it was necessary." He raised her hand and placed a tender kiss in the center of her palm. "Let us stop this talk. I think we need a change of venue to organize our thoughts. We should head to Sant'Anna for the weekend. The jet lag must be catching up with you and you must be tired. Come home with me. You can relax, and we will discuss all this in the morning."

"No." She had to be alone, and she had to think the situation through. "Plus, there is Cosmo to consider. We truly have so much work to do."

"If you must work, invite your friend, or legal representative, to stay in the guest bungalow." Pinching the bridge of his nose, he scanned the room. "You can work from the house, not sequestered in a hotel in the middle of Naples with you advisor."

Still, the status quo would persist if she returned to Positano. Not an option.

"Thank you, but it won't do this weekend." Sapphy twisted her hands in her lap. "What would Gabriella and your stepmother say?"

"Nothing. I will not tolerate them saying a thing."

She wanted to go home with Dante, and it was so hard to deny him. Damn. A deep, hollow pain settled in the center of her chest as disappointment registered on his face. He did not respond. Rather his gaze narrowed on hers. She could hear the questions he refused to ask looming between them, but she had started this game and needed to play by the rules.

"We'll leave it for now," she offered. "Let's talk about it on Monday. I'm going into the office in the morning, and I'd like to spend the night in the vicinity."

"It is not the safest place for a woman at night."

"I won't leave the hotel till morning."

Shrugging his concession, he reached for the leather case he'd brought with him.

"This is *our* complete contract." He unsnapped the locks and pulled out a file. "I had not read it since the morning of our wedding, but I reviewed it tonight since there appeared to be issues that concerned you. I discovered nothing new. Our fathers formed the company a month after the accident that took our mothers. It was so ironic how our fathers, who were much older than our mothers, outlived them. But, they did."

She nodded. Born to a father, who biologically was old enough to be her grandfather, her dad had always called her a gift that God gave him in his older years.

"You and I grew up together," he continued. "When your father was ill, he suggested the wedding contract for your protection. You agreed. We both agreed."

"I was only seventeen. I wasn't aware of the consequences."

"Consequences?" His face colored. Instantly, his jaw squared and the tiny muscle in the center of his cheek twitched.

Sapphy hadn't meant to sound accusatory, but she had. She placed her hand over his and rubbed the back of his wrist as he caressed her face. The heat of his touch burned a path to her soul as he ran his fingers over her cheek.

"There is no hidden agenda, *bambolina*. We remain married to protect the company interests until you turn twenty-three. At that point, we are each free to do as we please with our lives."

As if he had a conversation like this on a daily basis, he raised his shoulders and made a smacking sound with his lips. "If we chose to divorce and remarry, we can either continue with the company as it is, or disband it and split the assets evenly. Neither one of us will gain any more than the other."

"I'm aware of the terms." It didn't mean she liked them, but she knew them well. Nothing had been done without her knowledge. Contrary to her earlier statement, she'd entered into the arrangement well aware of the circumstances and of her free will. Now, she had to deal with the end.

"I'm really tired, Dante," she said, pulling the throw over her shoulders and snuggling into it. "You can sleep here tonight. The suite has a second bedroom."

"And where is your friend?"

"Cosmo is a night owl. He'd keep me awake all night if he stayed in here," she answered, and then recognized Dante's reason for asking. "He has his own room down the hall."

Dante's features relaxed. "It is the weekend. Your work should wait till Monday, but if you insist on starting immediately, you have all the keys and codes for headquarters. Use my desk until arrangements are made for your own office."

"Thanks. I will."

"*Daccordo.* I will let you get some rest." He leaned across the space and kissed her forehead. "If you change your mind about Sant'Anna, I will send the helicopter for you. I do not feel the urgency of time nipping at my heels the way you do, so I will agree to our talk next week. First thing, next week."

Chapter Three

"I don't get it. SD should've secured this contract three times already." Sapphy shook her head and turned up her palms. "It seems each time we're about to reach an agreement, something keeps popping up. Now the ECL is requesting a second facility for future use? That's absurd."

After a long, restless night, Sapphy needed to concentrate in order to read between the lines of the reports. She couldn't afford to miss a thing if she was going to prove herself as a competent partner.

"Something isn't Kosher." Cosmo nodded his agreement. "There has to be foul play involved."

She flipped through the dossier and studied the remainder of the file. It truly didn't make sense. SD Holdings could manufacture the security chips necessary with technology they had in place and with in-house experts leading the teams. The current infrastructure allowed SD to not only mass-produce the product, but to do so in a very cost efficient manner. So why the delay? And why would anyone question SD's ability to expand production in the future?

"Our strength and stability is impeccable. Our

track record speaks for itself." Sapphy pointed to the papers scattered on the desk. "You'd think the ECL is being fed false information for not jumping on this."

"There has to be more we're not seeing," Cosmo said, scratching his head. "This can't be about SD's financial reputation or ability."

"Then what is it?"

"Something not related to the business aspect of this arrangement." Cosmo drummed his fingers and threw her a questioning glance. "Have you discussed this project with Dante?"

The mention of *his* name lodged a weight in the center of her chest. She wanted to ask him, to tell him everything, but she couldn't. It was time to prove herself in the company.

As far as the personal talk went, she needed to know where she stood with him. This time, it wasn't her apartment, but every item in her suitcase that had benefited from her sleepless night. Even her panties were perfectly pressed.

"I haven't had the chance to speak with Dante about it," Sapphy said. "I'd much rather review all the facts we can before I do that. After all, I'm supposed to be a freaking competent professional."

Cosmo's personal cellular rang, disrupting their conversation. Chuckling as he reached for the phone, he held up his right index finger asking Sapphy to wait.

"Hello?"

She returned her attention to the files. It felt weird going through Dante's office without him present, but he had always said that she was welcome there. It was Dante who had given her not only the keys the room and file cabinets, but the combinations to the safes. He'd insisted she should have access to everything if anything should ever happen to him.

She glanced at Cosmo, who had his back turned to her and was standing by the window. Her friend, deep in conversation with New York, kept nodding and asking his sister to explain. He'd be on the line for a while longer.

Picking up the phone on the desk, she dialed Santa Anna and asked to speak with Dante. She was informed that he had left over an hour ago. Therese offered to reach him and relay a message.

"No, it can keep. Let him know that I'm at the office. I forgot my phone on the nightstand this morning, and I don't want him to try and contact me on it. You know how he gets when he doesn't know the when, where, how, or why of anything and everything. He can reach me on his private line at headquarters. I'll answer if it rings." Sapphy said goodbye to Therese and returned the handset to its cradle.

Dante's concern over her well-being had always comforted her in the past. It was an intimate safety net to know that he cared enough to ask after her. The last few weeks, she'd minimized his efforts with every chance she had. Each time he'd ask, 'How are things going?' She'd answer a simple, 'Good.'

Suddenly, she felt a tinge of guilt about her recent omissions of facts.

Cosmo flipped his phone shut and rubbed his forehead. "There have been some developments—"

"I was thinking," she blurted out. "I need to come clean with Dante before we can move on. It was wrong not to clarify my situation and plans over the past month. You know, I was out of school. He kept sending me all that money."

"It was your money, Sapphy."

She bit her lip and looked away.

"Listen to me," Cosmo continued in a hurried

manner, taking the seat in front of her. "You need to remain cool and collected if you want to succeed; both in your professional and personal life. There is no question that he's attracted to you. However, something is keeping him from allowing his feelings to surface."

"Perhaps lust—oops, I mean love—for his gorgeous stepsister?" The ugly green head of envy settled in her gut. She despised the heaviness and negativity the hideous persona added to her psyche, but no matter how she tried to stop it, she couldn't.

"I don't know." Cosmo shrugged, leaning across the desk and refusing to let her minimize the seriousness of the discussion. "Dante is not your keeper any longer. He may have been conscientious enough to see that your education was completed and that your company was safe, but today, that responsibility falls on you. Even by the conditions in your fathers' wills, you can go your separate ways in very short time."

"He wouldn't abandon me. He is my husband."

"No," Cosmo answered, shaking his head. "He is your business partner. Your marriage is only on paper."

She covered her ears and shook her head. She didn't want to hear this. Swiveling her chair, she stood and walked around the desk, recovering from the momentary lapse in strength.

"I'm aware of what needs to happen. So, on to other topics," she said, leaning on the desk. "Tell me what the call was about?"

Cosmo checked his watch.

"I have to go," he exclaimed, jumping to his feet and packing his case. "If you don't mind, please ask the hotel staff to collect my things and either send them to me or just hold on to them until I return."

"Your things?"

Where was he going? She needed his input. Her heart raced as if she'd run a marathon and her palms grew clammy. She wasn't ready for him to go. They hadn't even started their work, and she valued his insight on the legalities of the business transactions.

"I didn't realize the time. I have a flight to catch in ninety minutes." Searching his briefcase, Cosmo pulled out his passport and tucked it in the inside pocket of his jacket.

"What are you talking about?"

"It's not good," he said, securing the snaps and slinging the bag over his shoulder. He leaned in and gave her a quick peck on the cheek. "My father is in the hospital. He had another one of his dizzy spells and fell. He's bruised up, but nothing is broken. I need to get back and look after things."

"I understand," she whispered, burying the disappointment of his departure. "I'm going to miss you." Stepping forward, she wrapped her arms around her friend. "You're my secret power, my strength, and I thank you from the bottom of my heart."

"You're so much stronger than you know. You'll do fine without me. You're the mastermind here." He chuckled and framed her face with his hands, giving her an encouraging smile.

"I love you," Cosmo said, bringing his lips to her forehead.

"Love you, too," she whispered, letting her lashes drop.

A forced cough sounded from the other end of the room.

"Am I interrupting?"

Her eyes shot open. There was Dante, scowling and standing inside the office with legs slightly spread and arms crossed over his chest in a very combative stance. His gaze darted from Sapphy to Cosmo, his nostrils flared, and a crimson color flushed his neck.

"No." Cosmo released her and adjusted his case. "We were just saying goodbye."

"Yes," she said, taking a step back from her friend. "Cosmo has an emergency he needs to attend to back in New York. He must leave immediately and catch the next plane out."

Dante stalked across the office and stood beside Sapphy. Wrapping his left arm around her waist as his right arm jutted forward, he offered Cosmo his hand.

"Have a good flight," he said, his jaw clamped.

Cosmo let out a sharp breath, but accepted Dante's hand. "Thank you." Then, he turned to Sapphy. "I'll be back as soon as things are under control and Dad is comfortable at home."

She squirmed out of Dante's grip and rubbed the hip her husband had crushed against his side. Sapphy followed Cosmo to the door. "Call me when you land in JFK."

"Will do." Cosmo pretended to tip his hat and hurried to the elevator.

Preparing to give Dante a piece of her mind over the way he'd treated Cosmo, Sapphy turned on her heels and collided with a wall of muscle. Her hands sprawled over his chest so that she could maintain her balance, but the strong beating of his heart had an adverse effect. Startled and amazed at his demeanor, she found it hard to breathe. Strong determined arms wrapped around her, and he eliminated any space between them as he brought his body against hers and shivers ricocheted from the points of connection. The veins on his neck bulged and she craved running her fingers over them to feel his pulse.

More physical contact. More palpitations. More heat.

He didn't back away. His breath, hot on her face, made her want to melt into against him.

"Only yesterday, you claimed not to want to air dirty laundry in public." The intonation of his voice immobilized her. "Today, you stand in a place of business, entwined in the arms of a different man."

She shook her head. "It's not like that. Cosmo is a friend. A friend who just received horrible—"

"You cannot believe for a minute that any man could have you so close to him and not want you."

Huffing out some air, she pushed against his chest and locked her elbows, attempting to regain her composure. His accusation was ridiculous, the proof being Dante himself. He was close, and he didn't want her. He had nothing but anger for her.

"It is not that way—"

"Excuses, Sapphy?"

"No one even saw us."

"I do not believe that a man and woman who are not blood relatives could have a platonic relationship like you claim to have with Cosmo." His fingers relaxed considerably, but he did not drop his hands. "I am not blind. I may have had an obligation to fulfill these years, but my wife won't make a fool of me. You will act in an appropriate manner and not flaunt your relationships with other men. Cosmo is flesh and blood man," he continued in a gruff voice. "A man who is not immune to your sex appeal and beauty."

What she really wanted to ask was how he felt about her appeal and beauty, but she couldn't. Shocked by the anger embedded in his eyes, Sapphy shook her head.

"It was just a simple kiss goodbye."

He answered immediately, lowering his head and capturing her mouth. The kiss was not soft and sensuous. It wasn't a slow, seductive bonding. Rather, it was a hard, rough, almost punishing ecstasy she wished would never end.

Arching her back, she met his body and parted her lips to intensify the joining. His tongue invaded her starving mouth, and his rock-hard torso pushed against hers. With a muscular thigh between her trembling legs, he led her backward until she was up against the door and unable to move with the doorknob pushing into her backside.

Time stopped. She was lost. Then, as if spinning her on a wild amusement park ride, he abruptly ended the kiss and dropped his hands to clasp her hips.

"If you want to be kissed by a man, your husband will do it." He was half an inch from her burning lips, but his presence scorched. "And if you want to kiss a man, you will kiss only your husband." His gaze dipped from her eyes to her mouth, then back again. "*Capicci?*"

Sapphy nodded.

She understood.

"As you so kindly pointed out yesterday, we are now living in the same city." Dante turned his back and walked away, leaving her pinned by invisible hands to the hard wooden surface of the door, alone and exposed, without the shelter of his body.

She sighed and rubbed the bumps on her arms. Licking her lips, she savored the remnants of his taste and hungered for more. A single kiss from the damn man set an inferno ablaze inside her and she blinked repeatedly, attempting to see straight.

"We are married, and will remain as such for the next two months," Dante said, but didn't turn to look at her. "There is no room for disgracing our reputations. Not yours. Not mine. We will be seen together, and for all the eyes that will intensely follow us, we will be a single unit, cemented by our intense commitment to each other. There will be no question that you are my devoted and loving wife as much as I am your adoring and loving husband."

So the kiss meant nothing to him. He was testing her and being an overbearing chauvinist who wanted control of the situation. His objective was to make their marriage appear proper for other people to believe in their union.

"You will accompany me to social functions as my wife. You will work beside me as my partner, and I will teach you what you must learn in order not be taken advantage of in the industry." He turned his dark gaze on her, and the sensuous visual caress reached every inch of her body. "Basically, for the next few weeks, you will be attached to my side."

It wasn't how she'd intended for all of it to happen, but it would suffice. Dante was the best person to learn from, and he was the only one that wouldn't mislead her. She'd ignore her own needs and concentrate on the business. But her pride couldn't let everything go.

"There is no need for a mistress."

"What was that?" Dante asked.

She had thought aloud! Horrified, but unwilling to compromise on this detail, she raised her face and looked into his eyes.

"I will agree to your conditions. They are logical and serve our purpose well. However, you cannot keep a mistress. Not in the public's view, and not hidden from it. I will not be ridiculed and talked about."

"I accept." A mischievous gleam filled his gaze.

"No mistress. No other woman. No one, but you."

Releasing her breath, she smiled, returning to the desk and sitting in front of the files she'd been studying. Might as well get to work and not waste time.

"Fine," she said. "I have a few questions for you."

Fighting the effect of the kiss, she pointed to the papers, and desperately tried to calm the exhilaration throbbing through her body. She would manage to make him love her...one step at a time. Her plan of assuming her place in her father's company had just expanded to include taking her place beside her husband. They'd be a team, and together, they would go forward.

"What is the story with this deal?" She'd start with the financial interests they shared. "It seems like a perfect opportunity. Yet, the ECL has not signed off."

It took Dante a few moments, but he came next to her and placed a hand on the back of her chair. Nothing seemed to rattle him. He was cool as ice.

"As you could see from the reports, their hesitation has nothing to do with the business merits of our company," Dante replied, leaning over her and pointing out the stats.

It certainly didn't have to do with SD Holding's reputation or financial strength. Both were superior to the competition.

"We have the resources," he continued. "We have the talent. We have the ability to grow this project in a very easy and profitable manner."

His masculine scent was really getting to her. The office was unbearably warm. She lifted her hair off her neck and moved it to the opposite side from where he stood.

"Antonio and I have attempted to analyze and

comprehend this irrational delay," he said, gently sweeping a stray tendril of her hair into the pile she'd created. "There is some other force at play here."

"What do you mean?" Sapphy asked, surprised by the troubled sound of his voice. "Other forces not pertaining to business?"

"Honestly, some transactions are gray and we must use our instincts to make the final decision." He shook his head, as if in disagreement with his own words. "That is not the case in this situation. The positive potential heavily outnumbers any risk. There is no gray. It is black and white and a win-win situation."

"Then what is the problem?"

"The woman responsible for the final decision is a crude and harsh executive who takes her time in answering. But as you said, this is a deal that is too good to pass on. It does not make sense."

His heated touch lingered at the base of her nape, and she yearned to snuggle against his hand, to turn her face and kiss the center of his palm. The taste of him was still on her lips, and she couldn't help but run her tongue over them. In truth, she wanted the same heat, those same hands all over her body, caressing her worries away and assuring her that years of sensual pleasures awaited her.

"The ECL's benefit is obvious and it is in their benefit to commit." His strong, business voice broke through her dreamy existence. "She must have an ulterior motive in not jumping at this contract, because she is no idiot. Veronique Gautier is a sharp businesswoman who would not play with a decision like this. She must have information she doesn't agree with."

"Do you think there is a mole within our company

sabotaging this contract?" Sapphy asked, squeezing her legs to minimize the sensation building between them against her will. She attempted to sound professional, not like a woman lusting after the man beside her.

"We considered that." Dante pulled up a chair and sat beside her. "But there is nothing that can be 'leaked' to make us look bad. We can't figure it out." He patted her hand. "Your female intuition may give us a glimpse at her motives tonight."

"Tonight?"

"Yes. She'll be at a fundraiser we'll be attending."

He wasn't serious. Was he?

Reality settled about her, and the idealism of the sensual haze that she had been engulfed in evaporated. Surely, he didn't expect her to be ready on such short notice. She hadn't planned on a fancy social function her first weekend in Naples and she wasn't prepared. There was no way she could go.

"It is a fund-raising ball for the new children's hospital," Dante explained. "Giardetti Industries is hosting the event, and everybody who's anybody will be there. You'll accompany me, but if you feel intimidated about not knowing anyone, Gabriella will be there as well. She can help put you at ease with some of the attendees if for some reason I become otherwise engaged."

"Thanks, but no. It's the same if I attend personally or you represent both of us." In spite of her grand scheme, she wasn't ready to be with him in that type of social setting—especially not with another woman like Gabriella present. Sapphy wasn't a third wheel. "I'm sure the contribution you've made is very generous."

Logically, she had no right to be possessive of Dante. In the past, he had promised her protection and guidance, not his fidelity in the bedroom. He'd made that exclusive commitment to her only minutes earlier.

"Besides, I'd like to continue my review of these files. I don't have time for a party," she added.

"It was not a request. You *are* accompanying me tonight." He spoke in Italian. It was easy for the two of them to switch back and forth between languages, but Sapphy knew that he did this when he felt passionate about something. He wanted her to attend and wouldn't take no for an answer.

"Didn't you say that Gabriella is going?" That despicable feeling in her gut was back. She rubbed her belly.

"I will be attending the event with you. Gabriella will be there of her own accord." Dante pushed back his chair, stood, leaned over her, and then gathered the papers into a neat pile.

She bit her lower lip as he reached across her, the back of his arm grazing the front of her chest. Instantly, her nipples hardened at the light contact, and she prayed that he didn't notice as he dropped the file into the top drawer and locked it. She shifted, allowing him more room.

"*Andiamo,*" he said, inviting her to stand.

"Where?" She stared at him. "Where are we going?"

He grinned and took her hand. "First, we eat. Then, we'll go back to the penthouse and rest before the party." He helped her up from her seat. "It will be a waste of time to go to Positano only to return to the city tonight."

"I can't go," she argued. "I don't have any formalwear in Naples, and the stores will close soon."

Sapphy struggled to keep up with him as he gathered her belongings and led her out of the office.

"I'll take care of that. Besides, this is not your typically, stuffy ball. The party is at Massimo's, one of the trendiest spots in the city." He pushed the elevator call button and settled his hand in the center of her lower back. "Now tell me, *tesoro*, where would you like to eat?"

Tesoro? At least she'd graduated from a *bambolina* to a treasure. Her heart gave a little hop. On the outside, she smiled and laced her arm through his. If this was going to work, she couldn't expect everything to go smoothly. She had to roll with the punches.

"Your choice, Dante."

"*Buono.*"

The elevator door opened and they stepped inside.

Dante settled his hand on her hip and leaned close to her. His warmth engulfing her and spurring excitement and fear in her core.

"Trust me, Sapphy. I'll see to it that things work out."

Chapter Four

Dante and his wife may have been eating pizza, Sapphy's favorite food, but sitting at the corner table on the restaurant's patio was nothing short of majestic.

The bay sprawled beneath them, and the tall, sturdy walls of *Castell dell'Ovo* beckoned for them to slow down and enjoy the time and place in history that they shared. The sun's rays danced on the gold of the stone wall, glittering in the blue background of the bay. The afternoon was pure inspiration for the artists, lining the wall with their easels and crowding the pedestrians' path.

"What if the story of Virgil's egg is true?" Sapphy asked.

Dante laughed and stretched his legs as he leaned back in his seat. "A castle built on a magical egg?"

"Can you imagine if that egg broke after all these years? What a stench," she said, bringing a forkful of pizza to her mouth.

"You haven't changed, *bambolina*." He laughed loud, enjoying her take on reality. Voicing the most adorable thoughts, Sapphy had always managed to lift his spirits.

"*Bambolina*?" she asked.

Squaring her shoulders, she sat upright, and adjusted her posture. *Accidenti*, he'd made her uncomfortable and broken the intimacy that had temporarily settled between them.

"I did not mean to demean or belittle you." He reached across the table and covered her hand. "You are wonderful, and you never fail to make me laugh, Sapphy. I've missed that."

He could be patient. If he played his part properly, it would be easier for her accept her role. After all, he had too much invested in their relationship and company to let it fall away.

"Tonight, I'll have you rolling with laughter, especially when I show up to the ball dressed like Cinderella," she said, when the waiter approached with more wine. "You know, before her fairy godmother appeared."

"You'll look beautiful. As usual. You'll be the Belle of the Ball, and I'm willing to chase you down and fit those *Ferragamos* on to your feet," he drawled, and then checked his text messages. "I believe your fairy godmother is delivering your gown as we speak."

"Wow, Dante. You've done a one-eighty in less than an hour." A smile lit up her gorgeous face as she teased him. "Your dark and dangerous mood disappeared, and you're spinning fairy tales. I have no clothes, no makeup, not even my favorite perfume with me. Still, you're speaking of fairy godmothers and balls, and you're insisting I attend. What's up?"

"Nothing. This is just the way it has to be." He watched a concerned look replace her glowing smile, but he wasn't about to spoil the surprise and put her mind to rest. "Not only will we appear like a married couple should, but I'm looking forward to spending time together, enjoying your company, and catching up on what has happened since the last time we talked." And that had been years. "Truly talked."

"Then, I'll repeat the warning. I'm not prepared," she said, scraping gleaming white teeth over her bottom lip. "It won't be a glamorous first appearance for us as a couple. Not unless we go shopping immediately."

"Honestly, Sapphy. There is no need." Surprise or not, he couldn't let her fret over details. "I've requested the top collection from one of Naples's latest designers be delivered to the penthouse."

Shaking her head, she pressed her full lips and wet them. A small smile curled on her moist mouth, and she leaned her head to the side. She was gorgeous. Her ebony hair reflected the sunlight as her blue eyes sparkled. Sapphires—the most expensive and unique of the world's gems, much like the woman who carried their name.

They sat silently for a while, eating their lunch. Had he been too hard on her in the office? Had he demanded too much, too soon?

No. He deserved to have her on his arm when he wanted her. He'd stood by her better than most husbands did these days. She owed him the courtesy of reciprocating his years of attention with a few months of commitment to him.

Suddenly, she laughed.

Puzzled, he upturned his hand and raised his brow.

"If you picked out the dress, I'm sure to look like Mary Poppins. Did you order a matching hat?"

He was at a loss for words. She went from quiet and pensive to amused and jovial in three forkfuls.

"You don't remember, do you?" Sapphy asked as she tossed her dark mane over her shoulder.

"Mary Poop-ins? The movie?"

"Poppins," she corrected, lowering her fork and knife beside her plate. She placed her elbows on the table and rested her chin on her intertwined fingers. "It was a week before my fifteenth birthday. Katerina and I had snuck from the house for a night out."

"Katerina?" Dante remembered the spirited girl well. "She was a handful of trouble."

Sapphy nodded. "Anyway, we got all dressed up. We did our makeup, put on high heels, and walked three kilometers to *Stella D'Oro*. We had finally made our way to the bar when you appeared, threw a jacked over my shoulders and dragged me back home. Threatening to tell my father if you ever saw me at that club again, you locked me in my room and left."

The night flashed vividly in his mind. It had been the first time he'd seen her as the brightest star in a sea of women. His friends had made numerous comments about getting in good with the new girl, referring to her as *che bella, donna bellazza, che befana,* and when Dante had looked, he'd been shocked to see his own Sapphy surrounded by eager men at the bar. He'd bloodied his fist on his friend's lip for an inappropriate remark, hurried to her side, dropped his jacket on her shoulders to cover her flourishing body, and insisted on taking her home and away from the male hormones she'd set ablaze.

"You were fourteen, and it was two in the morning. You had walked into one of the area's hottest nightclubs, and it was full of people much more experienced than you were. How would you of handled yourself if a drunk, and much older, man put his hands on you and tried to get under that belt you called a dress?"

"I knew you were there." Sipping on her wine, she

shrugged and glanced over her glass at him. "I wasn't scared. I was just trying to see the type of reaction I'd draw."

"You did *draw* an impressive reaction. You most certainly made an impression." Dante had to fight his friends to keep them away from her. After he'd dropped her at Sant'Anna and returned to the club, he'd spent the night explaining that Sapphy was only fourteen and far too young for any of the men to be thinking of her as a potential lover.

"I embarrassed you that night." She dropped her gaze to her drink. "I was scared to come out of my room for over a week."

Chuckling, he leaned back in his seat and crossed his arms over his chest. "It kept you out of trouble." He smiled with the remembrance of what was said when he'd returned to the club without her. "Underage trouble was exactly what you were for all those suitors who had lined up to gain your attention. You didn't even have a clue about the commotion you created that night."

Finishing his wine, he pushed his plate forward. She still had no clue about the effect she had on men. Her dark pupils were big in the blue pools of her eyes. Tapping a long finger over her lips, she shifted in her chair, as if it was no big deal that she was absolutely breathtaking.

"Are you ready to go?" he asked.

"When you are," she replied in a soft voice.

So beautiful and no longer too young. Before him sat a grown woman, much more alluring than the girl at *Stella D'Oro*, but the same protective feelings that had ruled his actions almost a decade ago resurfaced. She was the most attractive woman in the restaurant, and she hadn't even noticed all the appreciative glances the other men gave her.

Bellisima.

The difference was that today, his possessiveness mingled with the pride he felt about having her on his arm as his wife—at least for the next two months.

"And Sapphy, you've never embarrassed me. I took you home so that I could keep you to myself."

* * * *

Entering the master bedroom, Sapphy released an awed breath as she spied three gowns strewn across the large bed.

"I feel like the princess you described at the restaurant," she whispered.

"You approve?" Dante asked from behind her.

"Approve?" She strolled over to the dresses and looked down, not daring to touch any of them lest she leave a mark on one. "They're gorgeous."

He walked up beside her and bent over the gowns, indicating the sexy gold one. "I think this one is my favorite."

"It looks a bit daring." She'd have less on than she did when she went to bed if she wore the gold dress. Considering the possible reaction she'd draw from Dante, a thrill ran through her body and settled at the juncture of her thighs. She was instantly damp imaging his body covering hers, his hardness pressed against welcoming softness, and his lips kissing her exposed cleavage.

"Try them all and pick whichever one you want. Matching shoes should be lined up on your side of the closet, along with the remainder of your clothes."

"My side of the closet?" Her heart beat so hard, and her pounding pulse collected in and closed off her throat.

"Do you think it would have been appropriate to

request that the staff set up the guest bedroom for my wife?"

Was he implying that she'd be sleeping in his bed?

The thought excited and terrified her at the same time. Dante was a man with discriminating taste and a lot of experience. Pretending to be sophisticated and worldly would not be enough. Her business, her marriage, and even her heart were at stake, and Sapphy had no experience to rely on for any of it.

"Sapphy, if we are going to live in the same city as husband and wife, we cannot allow any suspicion about our true relationship. We are lovers, reunited after months apart, and we must be completely taken with each other." He picked up the blue dress. "This is nice."

Apprehension chipped away at her heart. He was concerned about how they appeared to others. His comments were not motivated by his personal feelings, rather he did what he thought was proper for the relationship they were *supposed* to have.

Taking the exquisite gown from his grasp, she gathered the other two dresses and walked over to the closet, diverting her gaze. She didn't want him to see the disappointment in her eyes. He hadn't arranged for her to be in his bedroom because he wanted her in his bed; he simply wanted to save face for the staff's sake.

"So where will I *really* sleep?" Sapphy glanced over her shoulder, shuddering when he grinned casually.

He was perfect. Handsome, successful, and just the man she dreamt of. But, and here was the problem, he didn't see or want her as a woman.

"Right here."

He shrugged. It was a given.

"If necessary, I will figure out something else," he added, clearing his throat.

"Dante, this is ridiculous. Just because you've arranged for the gown and shoes doesn't mean I could prepare for tonight without my essentials. A woman needs more than an outer layer of clothing."

"You will find everything you need in the suite." Placing a big hand on her arm, he turned her to look at him. "Makeup, toiletries, and anything else a woman requires. You have no excuse not to join me tonight."

His mood had changed again, and Dante was confusing her more with each moment that passed. His eyes darkened, his chin squared, and the little muscle in the center of his jaw twitched. His determination was obvious, but the confusing thing was that he looked so amazingly attractive, in spite of his anger.

Why did she find him so appealing when she should be upset with the arrogant man?

"You will join me," he said, strutting toward the exit.

Swallowing her pride, she accepted his demand. She had to make that united appearance and play the part of the loving wife. Being seen together strengthened their company's reputation and afforded her the opportunity to meet the French woman. Sapphy needed to take a lesson from Dante: Being professional means putting personal baggage on hold.

"If you care for an afternoon coffee, I'll be on the terrace. If not, be ready by eight. The car will arrive at that time to deliver us to the fundraiser." Taking his hormonal mood swings with him, he disappeared out the door and let it swing shut behind him.

Not bothering to speak because he didn't wait for her to reply, Sapphy stared at the dark wood for a good thirty seconds before shaking her head to clear it. Like an intruder, in what was supposed to be her own room, she pulled open drawers to discover women's clothing in her size. There were matching lace panties and bras, silk lingerie, casual t-shirts, jeans, workout outfits, and business suits in the closet. Next, she checked the en-suite bath, only to find it complete with three different lines of makeup, her own brand of shampoo and conditioner, and even the correct deodorant.

"Always efficient and complete," she said, sighing and dropping to the seat at the vanity table. He'd gone through a lot of trouble for appearance's sake. She was only here for a night or two, and by the designer labels gracing her new clothes, it was going to be a very expensive weekend.

She'd make every cent count. Because, even if he claimed this was all for the perception of a proper marriage, the kiss he'd scalded into her soul had been in private.

* * * *

"You are lovely," Dante breathed, settling against the limousine's soft leather.

"Thank you," she replied, turning in her seat and adjusting his tie. "You don't look too shabby yourself."

Her dark hair pulled loosely from her face, rested high on her head, with a few tendrils strategically allowed to fall over her neck. Adorned in a simple, yet thick, gold knotted necklace and long matching earrings, she wore no other jewelry.

The driver made a left and pulled up to the elaborate guest entrance of the palazzo. When the employee left them alone and exited to come around and open their door, Dante brushed the side of her cheek with the back of his hand. He couldn't help himself. Sapphy was so beautiful. He struggled to keep his libido under control, but it would be impossible if she continued to touch him through the night. He didn't want to rush her and ruin their chances at a physical relationship.

"Tonight's function is being hosted by one of Italy's most influential building conglomerates. Not only is Giardetti raising funds to add a hospitality wing to the new children's hospital for family members while the kids receive long-term treatments, but he is raising awareness of the growing problems our inner city youth are facing," he said. The driver reached the door. "So, put a big, glamorous smile on your face and attract as many photographers as you can. This is a very noteworthy and noble event."

"I have no doubt," she said in a cool tone, as the door swung open. "Have we made our contribution yet?"

Nodding, Dante climbed out and offered her his hand.

"Good. Any occasion to benefit children is a worthy cause."

"Yes, anything for the children," he repeated. However, his thoughts were anywhere but on the night's event. Mesmerized by her lips, he focused on their shine and hungered to taste them again. The kiss they'd shared in the office had lit a fire that he had been unable to extinguish, regardless of the responsibility he'd attempted to push to the forefront.

He closed his hand possessively around hers and held it tight, cupping her elbow and pulling her closer. He tried to tell himself it was pure sexual frustration because of the agreement they'd made that afternoon. Any mandated restriction made the task of celibacy seem impossible.

Since he was to be faithful to their vows, and he had agreed not to consider anyone other than her as long as they remained married, he had to keep things in the proper perspective. He might want her, he could demand her, but what would the benefit be if she weren't willing?

"You're in a serious mood. Very pensive," she said, as they approached the red-carpeted entrance. "Is something wrong?"

"No, no. I was just thinking about the night ahead."

"Don't worry. I won't embarrass you—again." She smiled regally as they stepped through the palazzo's grand entrance. "I know how to behave in public."

The problem is not you, tesoro. How will I behave? How can I have you so close and restrain myself?

"I have no doubt you'll charm those stiffs," he said, attempting to lighten the mood. Dropping his hold on her elbow, he crooked his arm. "Shall we mingle?"

She laced her arm though his and took an audible breath. "Ready."

"And, Sapphy," he added, stepping on the carpeted walkway. "You could never embarrass me."

Inside the elaborately decorated club, Dante rested his hand on her bare back and fought the urge to wrap up his wife and take her back home. The sultry and sensuous décor did nothing to appease his body's frustration.

Envisioning her sculpted naked form against the shimmering cloth, strategically strewn between the decorative columns to add the illusion of clouds, his mind filled with images of lovemaking in a secluded heaven. The gold of her dress shimmered under the illuminated red floor lamps and gave off a decadent glow. The addition of sultry jazz in the background and the guests coupled on the dance floor only intensified the longing he felt to make their marriage real in every sense. His patience for her to come to the same realization as he held dissipated with each note the saxophone played.

For him, Sapphy was temptation personified. The dress draped over her perfect body, covering the essentials in an enticing and provocative manner. Tying around her neck, the silk material exposed her back and concealed only her rounded bottom and legs as it swayed with each step she took. From the front, two long pieces of fabric travelled vertically over her breasts, converging low on her tight, flat stomach. There was more than a little of her smooth and tanned skin in sight, and he grew more protective with each glance coming their way from the other guests.

How was he expected to last with her beside him for two months?

She continued to smile as they walked through the room together and accepted drinks from the waiter's tray. The club's fixtures, meant to entice the patrons into a fantasy world of ecstasy and wanton indulgences, did their job perfectly.

"To my wife," he said, raising his glass. "To an incredible evening."

"I do hope you're enjoying yourselves," a familiar voice sounded from behind them.

With a huge grin on his face, Luca Giardetti grasped Dante's hand and hit his upper arm. "Who is this lovely woman who is making you look so good tonight?"

"My beautiful wife." Liking the sound of his own words, Dante bowed and rolled his hand in an exaggerated motion to introduce her. "Sapphy, this GQ impersonator is Luca Giardetti of Giardetti Industries, our host and one of my best friends."

"At last," Luca said, raising Sapphy's hand to his lips. "I have the honor of meeting the woman who has held my friend's heart captive all these years." He brushed his lips over the tip of her knuckles.

"More like a treat," Dante added, peeling Luca's fingers off of Sapphy's. "Don't you have some host duty to attend to?"

Laughter erupted from both of the men, but it was the pride that flourished in Dante's chest that overwhelmed him. He looked at the beauty on his arm and placed a kiss on her cheek.

"You Italians are such masters of flattery," she said, gracing them with a big smile. "If I've held my husband's heart captive all this time, why haven't I met one of his dearest friends before now?"

What a multifaceted woman she was. She amazed him more with each minute that passed. Dante grinned and marveled at Sapphy's easy comeback and her spunk. She had them on this one, but Luca wasn't stumped by her response.

"Ah, *bella*, it was you who was so far away in that university across the sea." Luca raised his brow, setting many unanswered questions free to loiter in the air. "You and my own bride left us to become worldly scholars. We were two men in our circle of friends, with no lady at our side, left to fend for ourselves. We only had each other to escort to functions such as these. How do my blasé coffee-colored eyes compare to your sparkling blue ones? I think your husband missed gazing into those priceless treasures."

She gave a small curtsy, acknowledging that the other man was a good rival at word games. "A pleasure to meet you, Luca."

"The pleasure is all his," Dante kidded, sliding his palm over her silken back and spreading his fingers to cover more of her creamy skin.

Sapphy jumped at his touch, but he persisted and

feathered his fingers over her back until she relaxed against him. It took her a moment, but when she appeared to accept his touch with calm, it felt so natural. So right.

Business. Get control and keep it to business.

She'll come around.

Eventually.

"I'd like to introduce you to the woman who is hesitating on the contract we discussed earlier," Dante said against her ear.

Sapphy nodded, weaving her arm though Dante's and intertwining her fingers with his. "Yes, I'd like that."

Luca offered his hand to Dante, and then graciously placed a kiss on Sapphy's cheek.

"I see that Sapphyra is the complete package: beauty and brains." His friend leaned close and whispered, "You're a lucky man."

How is that I have her beside me, but she is still off limits? Answer me that, my friend.

"I know," was all he said aloud before excusing himself and leading Sapphy to Veronique Gautier.

Gautier was the stiffest of the stiffs in the large ballroom. The stark, bold, and intimidating French businesswoman met his gaze. She'd worked hard to cultivate a dynamic image for herself over the past decade. So hard, that it was difficult to imagine her having any fun. Too bad, Gautier had much to offer, but kept it all tucked away under her suit.

Everyone needed to let off steam occasionally; even a woman who had to prove herself over and over in a community of successful men.

Veronique was always a step ahead of the industry and blazed a trail for others to follow. Dante admired her insight and drive. The only time she'd faltered was two years earlier. Her husband had betrayed her in an international agreement she had been working on. The lowlife had been caught sharing information with, and sleeping with, the competition.

As if in a trance, the high-powered executive's sharp gaze fixed on Sapphy and did not waver as they made their way across the ballroom.

"Veronique, I'm so glad that you decided to attend," Dante said, raising the woman's hand to his lips.

"Once Luca's office called and explained the purpose behind the event, I couldn't stay away."

"Well, I'm happy you didn't." Dante grinned and took a step back. "Please allow me to introduce my wife, Sapphyra. Sapphyra, Miss Veronique Gautier."

"Pleased to meet you, Miss Gautier."

The women shook hands and exchanged polite smiles.

"Please call me Veronique." The French woman's face softened once the formal introduction was done.

"Veronique it is." His wife smiled radiantly, casting him a quick glance for confirmation on the casual tone. "And, you can call me Sapphy. Sapphyra is only for bill collectors and legal representatives."

"Dante, I don't think I've ever met your wife before." Veronique turned to face him, her eyes full of surprising warmth. "I didn't take you for the sort of man to isolate each part of your life and keep Sapphy away from the business end of things."

"Actually, Sapphy is my partner, both at home and in the office. She is the S in SD Holdings." He recalled the words Sapphy had used in the conference room and grinned, proud to claim ownership of the woman and the words.

A finely shaped dark brow arched on the French

woman's face with skepticism. "Come to think of it, I may have heard rumors of you being married from others, but you had never confirmed the fact. I am sorry, but I cannot recall meeting your wife."

"You're correct, Veronique," Sapphy interjected. "We haven't met." She then turned and gazed softly at Dante. "I haven't been around much."

With her big blue eyes fixed firmly on Dante, Sapphy stirred the embers of the fire she'd set in his body from the first moment she'd exited the bedroom. He shifted from one foot to the other in order to conceal the physical reaction to her intimate attention.

"Dante has been very supportive of me completing my education in the States. I've been in New York for a few years and unfortunately unable to accompany him on such occasions or do my share in the office." Sapphy rested her hand on his shoulder. "I've been extremely blessed to have such a chivalrous knight bearing both our burdens in the most generous fashion." She moved close and rested her body against his side, stoking the fire deep in his core. "But I'm here now, and he's stuck with me."

"Willingly, *cara mia.*" Dante lowered his head and brushed his lips against her temple. "Willingly."

"My husband is a very patient man. And, I'm a very lucky woman." Sapphy swept a hand over his jaw in a sensual touch.

Reveling in the intimacy between them, he settled his arm over her bare shoulders and gathered her possessively against his greedy body. He didn't care that they were in public. He didn't care if there was a certain type of behavior people expected of him at these sorts of functions. Dante wanted his wife.

A man had a right to his wife, didn't he?

Discussing the worthy cause they were supporting,

the glass ceilings women encountered in the corporate world, and the difficult balance that a woman needed to maintain between professional and personal lives, Sapphy and Veronique appeared like old friends catching up on time lost.

When Sapphy asked for some mineral water, he excused himself and walked to the bar. It was faster than catching a server's attention. Upon returning and offering her the drink, an excited Sapphy greeted him like a young teenager.

"Veronique has never been to Positano," his wife said.

"You really should make the time to see our little paradise," he replied in a polite tone. "We would enjoy having you visit and giving us the opportunity to extend our personal hospitality."

Sapphy's eyes gleamed with excitement. "She's coming down with us when we leave Naples next weekend."

Shocked, he didn't answer.

"Yes, thank you for the invitation." Veronique placed a hand over her chest. "Do not misunderstand, I love your country. But living in a hotel suite for almost a month is not the coziest way to get to know it. I would love to visit your home."

"We would love to have you," he said, swallowing the choking sensation in his throat.

Chapter Five

"Why did you do that?"

"Do what?" Sapphy shrugged, preceding Dante into the penthouse.

His easygoing public character vanished the moment they'd left the palazzo. Moving past her, shaking his head and balling his fist against his thigh, he turned and glared at her.

"You can't waltz in here and make moves that could jeopardize what I've been working on for all this time without consulting me." He spoke quickly and in Italian, taking her aback.

"Dante, I thought we had a nice time tonight. You seemed very relaxed while we were dancing and talking with your acquaintances."

"Exactly." He pinched the bridge of his nose. "Those people are acquaintances—business acquaintances. There only so much information about my personal life I like out in public. You can't go around opening us, and the company, to slander. It could be disastrous."

Slander? What was he talking about?

"Our relationship is not easily understood in the business world and may be misconstrued as a weakness in the company's foundation. Other than Luca, the people you met tonight are not privileged to personal information."

Sapphy strolled to where he stood, placed a hand on his jaw, and guided him to look directly at her. "You said Luca is a good friend of yours. Why wouldn't he know? As for anyone else, I don't see a problem with the way things went tonight."

"You don't see a problem?" He grasped her shoulders and pulled her near. "I do."

She remained silent, attempting to figure him out. Dante rarely got annoyed, rarely raised his voice, but now, he did both. This was a different side of him she'd never seen before.

"You need to slow down. Take some time to learn the details about the people we are dealing with, rather than assuming that everyone is what they appear to be. They're not all pleasant and admiring supporters," he said.

Her stomach twisted and unease crept over her. Dante was condescending again. They had shared a great evening, on par with each other emotionally and socially, but suddenly things changed. This roller coaster ride was making her nauseous.

Talking to her like a child, the frustration in his voice was evident and rang in her ears. His gaze grew darker with each word. His fingers, even though they didn't hurt her, were tight on her forearm.

Sapphy blinked back the tears and decided it was best to hear him out. She urged him to explain.

"Two years ago, Veronique went through a very public and nasty divorce. She is extremely critical of anything, anything, other than traditional relationships. The woman has very strong views on marriage and knowledge of our true connection could influence the contract. By inviting her into our home and private life, you practically threw open our bedroom door." Then he leaned closer, inches from her. "A bedroom we do not share." He let out a long breath. "How will that make us appear?"

The air escaped from the joyous balloon of the evening, and the happiness bubble dropped between them, flaccid and empty.

It was all about appearances with him. All about the correct presentation of their association as it pertained to SD Holdings. Did he forget that it was he who had insisted she accompany him as his wife?

"If we must, we'll share a room for the weekend," she retorted in an offhand manner.

"No, Sapphy! You're asking too much." He dropped his hold. Stepping away from her, he shook his head and huffed out his words. "You expect me to sleep beside you and act like everything is normal between us. I'm supposed to turn on my side and fall asleep as if I do it every night."

Did sleeping with her turn him off that much?

Just because she had little experience, didn't mean she was no good at it. She was a quick study and a determined participant. If he requested, she would sleep with him—in any sense of the word. If her body was tied to her inheritance, she might as well place it where her heart was...with Dante.

Thoughts raced through her mind as she studied his demeanor. They had never shared a bedroom before, but if only for a few months, they needed to start. Maybe those months could extend into years. Maybe he'd learn to desire her in a way that had a man yearning for a woman. And, maybe he'd grow to love her the way a man loved a wife.

Biting her lower lip, she walked up behind him.

Gathering confidence with each step, she placed her hand on his shoulder and held her breath. If only for two months, she would be his wife. She would handle the rejection when he let her go.

"I'm here, Dante. I'm ready to be yours in every sense of the word."

"We're not kids any longer. You're playing with fire." He faced her. "Fire burns, Sapphyra."

She'd never heard truer words.

His touch seared her skin. Heat filled her cheeks. Her heart hammered. She wanted Dante as her first lover. He was the only man she'd ever loved. If he was going to turn her away, she was surely going to have a meltdown.

He tangled his fingers in her hair and cupped her head, his palm scorching the base of her neck. The intensity displayed on his face shook her assurance, but he held her tight and didn't release her.

She wanted him.

She needed him.

There was nothing more right than being with him. Then, in a flash of logic, or perhaps as a means of defense, she put her personal needs aside and justified the physical intimacy as a requirement for the company to function properly. She'd guard her heart.

"I know," she breathed, raising her face and offering her trembling lips for him to take.

Dante's agonizing caresses marked her being. His proximity carved an aching need in her core to have more of him.

Desire burned in his eyes and his lips claimed hers, stirring the fervor brewing inside her to hurricane strength. With the turmoil raging between her body and psyche, she struggled to remain standing. His kiss, hot, demanding, and branding, stole her breath and left no doubt that he was going to collect on her wifely dues.

His intoxicating taste seeped into her mouth with each torturous stroke of his tongue across hers. She was lost. The air dissipated from the room, and her knees grew weak, as his arm wrapped around her waist and supported her weight.

Unable to think any longer, she pressed her sensitive breasts to his chest and the mere contact spread flames over every inch of her skin. Clearly not the time for her mind to take control, sensations and emotions were the only things at play in this liaison.

His hands sprawled down her lower back, cupping her rear and pulling her against him. Dante pressed the evidence of his excitement into her belly and intensified the passionate anticipation that had her world spinning. He was going to make love to her. He was going to complete her.

Tugging her hair loose, he moved her head back and commanded her to meet his eyes. "There is no going back."

It was a statement, but he meant it as a question. Dante was giving her a final opportunity to back away. She shook her head, and he gathered her into his arms and carried her into the master bedroom.

His lips, hot and urgent, ravaged the exposed areas of her body. Her skin sizzled and moisture pooled between her legs as his breath swept over her, and she knew she wanted this more than anything. Leaning her head on his shoulder, she inhaled his scent and placed small, wet kisses on the side of his neck.

Dante wasn't slow and patient. He pulled her arms above her head and clasped her wrists in one hand. Pressing her against the bedroom wall, he bent his head to suckle her breast over the gold material. His thigh nestled between her legs, intensifying the moist heat drenching her panties.

"You are magnificent," he breathed. "Even more important, you are all mine. I am going to make love to you until you can think of nothing but me."

Like anything else is possible.

"My name will be the only word on these luscious lips of yours, *bella*. You will call for me over and over as your body climaxes and aches for more of me."

With her hands still clasped above her head, her nipples jutted against her dress and strained for his kiss. She wasn't sure if she was doing it right, but she arched her back, asking for more of his attention. He brushed his lips over her breasts, sliding his hands to her abdomen. Slowly, too slowly, he raised her skirt and set her to rest against his thigh.

Her head fell back against the wall and he claimed her neck, stroking and licking at the sensitive skin, cooling and heating it simultaneously. Thankfully, he dropped his arm around her waist as he set her upright. Her trembling legs would not have supported her. With a bit of uneasiness, she touched his jaw and ran her hand along the strong lines of his chiseled face. The way the dark stubble felt on her fingertips emulated the sensation in her core: prickly, exciting, stimulating. She trembled with fear; she trembled with desire, but could not help but want more as his fingers released her wrists.

Removing his tie, he unbuttoned his collar and looked at her like a panther eyeing his prey. Dante bent his head and kissed her neck. This time soft, tender, and enticing scrapes of his teeth followed sensuous sweeps of his tongue over her needy skin. The dizzying swirls of passion and heat edged into her heart, and she trusted her body to Dante as she never before trusted anyone. She was his.

His erotic ministrations, so heavenly and new, settled on her breasts as his mouth traveled down the valley between them, leaving moist trails of promised ecstasy leading to the gold material she'd worn because of his earlier statement. Nudging the dress to the side, he freed the heavy globe and exposed her to the cool air.

Sapphy adjusted her stance and offered her aching nipple, but he prolonged the agony, tasting every bit of breast before taking the taught peak into his warm mouth.

Strong, expert fingers teased her other breast through the silk fabric as she ran her hands over his back and across his hips to his front. Finding his belt, she unbuckled it and pulled it off. Sapphy fumbled with his shirt buttons, but stilled her hands as his teeth grazed her exposed nipple. Abandoning her original mission, she inhaled deep and moaned aloud.

His mouth caressed her flesh and placed her in a sensual heaven she'd only dreamt about. Closing her eyes, she drifted in the emotional and physical warmth until her head refused to stop spinning from his exquisite attention.

Attempting to collect and compose herself, she tried with the buttons, but was unable to focus. He covered her hands.

"We're past the point of proper etiquette, *cara mia*," he said, pulling the shirt off his chest. Alabaster buttons pinged on the marble floor, and he threw the shirt across the room and kicked off his shoes.

She stared at his chest, rising and falling with obvious need for her. His trousers extended with desire, and she felt so out of her league. Other, more confident and experienced, women her age would not be intimidated, but she questioned her ability to please and satisfy him.

"I'm with you, *tesoro mio*. Passion takes two," he breathed as if reading her mind. "We will do this together, as one."

With shaky hands, Sapphy reached to release his erection, but he caught her wrist and raised it to his lips. Dante slowly kissed down the inside of her arm and tingles danced on her skin. Then, lifting the arm, as if it was a long, lost treasure, above her head and maneuvering her with gentle purpose, he made her pirouette ahead of him, commenting on her statuesque beauty. Keeping her arm raised, his gaze traveled over her body.

"You are the most beautiful woman in the world, *cara mia*," he drawled, shaking his head. "I am the most fortunate man in the world." Craving his attention, her nipples jutted higher. He didn't disappoint her. First, he suckled the bare one, and then the one straining against the silk dress.

"This won't do," he said, untying the halter style straps holding her dress in place.

The gold fabric pooled around her ankles, and he stepped back, removing his own clothing in a blur of movement as words of worship spilled from his lips. Joy and elations waltzed in Sapphy's core, her heart raced and was about to explode through her chest as she realized that his reaction was completely due to her presence.

"*Perfezione*," he whispered, letting out a long breath. "More than I could have ever imagined."

Sparks shot from the visual caress of her body and collected into an inferno at the juncture of her legs. The area covered by the lace triangle was private and special. She was no prude, but she had always wished that the first man she'd share her body with would be the one she loved. She loved Dante, so her wish was a reality. She squeezed her eyes tight and refused to think past the feel of his touch.

Sapphy did not move as he traced the thin strings of her panties with his finger and her core pulsed

"Soft, you are so soft." Dante's head dipped to her neck and his tongue meandered in a torturing dance down the side. "I cannot get enough of you." He twisted her and drew her back against his chest, chasing doubts of her sexual prowess away with the intensity of his touch as he held her against his body.

Sapphy let out a slight breath, and relief flowed over her as the words she needed to hear left his mouth and his hands continued the sensual exploration of her body. Encircled by his arms, she felt strong, beautiful, and capable.

"Your scent is intoxicating." Resting his chin on her shoulder, he slid his palms up her belly to cup her breasts. Rolling her nipples between his thumb pads and fingertips, he continued the assault of kisses on her neck. "You are like an addiction, and now that I've had a taste of you, I can't be without you." He was speaking in Italian, not censoring his words and speaking from deep inside. "I want you so bad. All of you. Immediately and now. But I promise to make it right our first time."

Rigid and searing with longing, his erection pressed against the soft flesh of her rear. She squirmed to fit her hand between them and encircled him with her fingers.

He was larger than she'd expected, harder that she'd imagined, and she closed her eyes, picturing him entering her.

"Sapphyra?"

"Yes," she whispered, keeping her eyes shut and savoring the touch of his fingers mingling in her damp curls.

"I have no protection," he groaned, slipping his finger over her moist folds and fondling her tiny nub. "But, I accept and welcome all the responsibility of our actions. I want you so much. I cannot let you go."

Biting her lower lip, she released her hold on his arm, and twisted to meet his dark gaze. "I'm prepared."

His silence posed the obvious questions of how and why, and she was compelled to deal with the reality of their relationship.

"I'm on the pill," she added, hoping he would not consider her promiscuous or loose.

His lips found hers and the sensual assault on her mouth resumed. Leading her to the bed, he guided her into the center of the plush mattress, and lowered the last piece of clothing over her thighs and down her legs. His fingers roamed down her chin, over her throat, and zigzagged across her body, in a slow trail to her toes.

"So soft, so smooth, so gorgeous, and so mine."

"Yours, Dante," she replied, arching her back and raising her hips to him. "Please, I can't wait any longer."

He groaned his response, joining her on the bed. Fitting himself between her thighs, the steely length his erection settled against her folds. When his smooth tip stroked the sensitive skin, marking the erotic juncture at the center of her core, it sent shockwaves of pleasure through her body.

Lowering his lips to hers, his tongue entered her mouth, simulating the movement of their hips as he pushed into her warmth. Greedily, her body took him and held him tight.

Dante was home—where he had longed to be, and she was his heaven on earth. He looked into her beautiful face, thanking God for making her.

"You fit, we fit," she breathed against his mouth.

"Perfectly," Dante answered, pushing a stray tendril hair away from her face and savoring her full lips as he ran his tongue over them.

Unable to restrain his need for her a moment longer, he raised her hips and drove deeper into her warmth. Sheathed inside his wife, he knew the world was at his feet. The power and strength he found intoxicated and encouraged him to love her more.

She was the ideal woman. All he'd dreamed. And she was his.

"Open your eyes, *cara mia*."

Sapphyra's dark lashes lifted, revealing the most precious sapphires in the world. Bluer than usual, her gaze reached into his soul and did things to his mind and body that no woman ever had.

She was his wife, he had a right to her, and she was with him. It didn't matter how long he'd waited for her to come to him willingly; she'd come.

He blanked out the logic and inhaled the scent of her excitement, the scent of their lovemaking. He'd make this the most pleasurable experience for her, and she'd never want to leave him.

Sapphy whimpered as he slowed the pace and reduced the friction between their bodies. Her big eyes questioned his motives.

"Relax," he whispered, reigning in his own enthusiasm. "We have all night, *amore mia*."

Her sweetness filled his mouth when he kissed her neck, then tasted each tender nipple. Relishing the sound of each moan escaping her lips, he prolonged the delight of their joining, and held her in his arms as her climax hit.

Cupping her head, he pressed her to his heart, and shivers traveled down his spine from the sensations her body imparted on his. Insistent on their first time being more than good, he patiently waited for her to return to him, and then started to once again move gently within her, encouraging her back to blissful heights and whispering words of his undeniable passion for her.

Finding an exotic rhythm, they moved together in perfect unison. Limbs and lips intertwined, he feasted on the gifts his wife bestowed on him. This time, when her climax began and she tightened around him, he threw back his head and joined her in a spiral of ecstasy like none other he'd ever experienced.

* * * *

Sapphy's arm sprawled across his heart, her pinky making small circles on his chest. Closing his fingers around her wrist, he raised her hand to his lips and placed a kiss in the center of her palm.

"*Comme sei bella*," he said, adjusting her to lie over his body as he looked into her eyes. Taking her face into his hands, he raised his head and kissed her full on her love-swollen lips. "Perfect."

"You're not so bad yourself," she said, gracing him with a divine smile and resting her cheek against his heart.

He stroked her gorgeous hair, caressed the length of her back, and willed the moment to continue. However, he couldn't help but wonder why she hadn't told him that she was a virgin. Her body had revealed the truth as he'd entered her, and he had to restrain himself from spilling over with excitement from his discovery.

Elated that she'd waited for him, Dante confirmed what he had known from the day he'd married her: Sapphy was his and only his. He was never going to let her go.

"*Cara mia*, why are you on the pill if you weren't sexually active?"

"I was coming home to you." She met his gaze, her eyes shining bright. "Like you said, we're not children any longer, Dante. And, like I said, I am here as your wife, in every capacity. I don't expect you to be celibate while you are by my side. It wouldn't be logical."

What did logic have to do with what they shared? A weight settled in the center of his chest.

"I see," was all he managed. Keeping his hand on the small valley above her rounded bottom, he pulled the sheet over them.

Sapphy settled against him, and he resisted the desire to question her any further. Within minutes, her slow, soft breathing told him that she'd fallen asleep.

For Dante, it wasn't that easy. Toying with the long hair splayed across his chest, he allowed the silky strands to slip through his fingers. The past few days replayed in his mind and kept him awake for hours.

If she hadn't come to him when she had, he would have gone after her. Time was running out on their agreement, and he wasn't willing to gamble and lose her forever. He was no longer the young, inexperienced man she'd married. Dante had proven himself and his worth. He deserved her. He wanted her. And, he would have her.

He'd worked hard to learn the trade and had solidified their company's place in the international arena. No one dared to question his integrity or power. He was the sort of man she deserved and the same type of man she'd told him she wanted to marry one day.

On that afternoon in the hospital chapel, he had promised her that he would take care of her. Then, he'd promised himself that he would wait for her to come to him. He had done just that. He had met his obligation.

No matter how or why, Sapphy was with him and in his bed. He wasn't letting her out.

Chapter Six

The continuous ring of the phone yanked Sapphy from a sweet dream. She reached across the empty bed and stretched for the receiver.

"*Pronto?*"

"*Buongiorno.* Sapphyra?"

"Yes." Sapphy wrinkled her nose at the sound of Carmella's voice. She rarely, if ever, received a call from her Step-Monster-In-Law. "Good morning. Are you looking for Dante?"

"Actually, may I speak with Gabriella?"

Sapphy pulled herself to a sitting position and covered her breasts with the sheet. Her confidence and bliss evaporated into the morning light.

"She's not here. Can I help you with something?"

"What do you mean she's not there?" Carmella's voice climbed an octave with the question. "I can't believe she's left with Dante for the weekend and didn't bother to tell me how I could contact her."

Taking a deep breath, Sapphy bit her lower lip and shook her head. She didn't want to know about Dante's weekend jaunts with Gabriella, but her step-monster-in-law rubbed her nose in the affair. Did the woman have no couth?

"Sapphyra?" The shrill voice wouldn't be quiet.

"One minute, please."

The door to the bathroom opened and Dante stepped out with a white towel knotted over his hip.

"*Buongiorno, bella.*" He strolled to the bed and placed a kiss atop her head while twisting his palm up in question.

Sapphy covered the mouthpiece. "It's your stepmother. She's looking for Gabriella."

Nodding, he took the phone from her hand. "*Buongiorno, Carmella. Come stai?*"

He sat on the edge of the mattress, trailing a finger down the side of Sapphy's face, over her neck, and bringing it to rest on the swell of her breast as he cupped her gently over the cotton barrier.

"*Sì.* I will have her call you as soon as possible." He grinned and slowly lowered the sheet. "*Sì, Carmella. Daccordo.*" Replacing the receiver on the cradle, he brought his lips to Sapphy's. "You are more beautiful each time I see you."

The ease in which he went from one conversation to the other stunned her. He didn't even blink from the discomfort of the situation. That was the difference from having a long line of lovers to only having one. Sapphy couldn't shift gears as easily.

"Your kiss-swollen lips and the traces of our lovemaking on your skin are so tantalizing that I don't want to let you get out of this bed."

"Thank you," she said, feeling her face heat with embarrassment. "I think."

"No, thank you." He sealed his lips on hers and sent ripples of electricity through her body. "I am so pleased that you have come home, Sapphy. We have a few months to get you ready to assume full responsibility for your position at SD. I do not believe it will take as long, and I do not worry about your abilities. But, you must know that I will always stand by you. I am just happy that I have you with me," he paused, closing his large hand over her fingers and pulling them to his chest. "To truly be with you."

Astonished, Sapphy stared into his dark eyes. He was sincere, heartfelt, and intimidating. She didn't know how to react to his comments, so she smiled and waited for him to make the next move.

Bracing himself on either side of her, he slowly lowered his mouth to hers. The minty taste lingering on his teeth made her tongue tingle, and she curled her toes as the feeling traveled through her body. He was a great lover. Attentive and gentle, he managed to ignite passion each time he touched her. Dante made her forget everything but him.

She should have been annoyed with the call that had so rudely awakened her. She should have asked him why Carmella had assumed Gabriella was with him. But she couldn't think past the pleasure of his erotic strokes over her skin. Instinctively, she raised her arms and entwined her fingers in his wet hair.

There was no doubt. She wanted Dante to stay with her. She needed him to touch her. And, she ached for him to fill her and reenact the scenarios that had exploded around them in the night.

"Making love in the morning has always been one of my secret fantasies," she breathed, arching her back and offering herself to the man of her dreams.

"You must list your fantasies," he said, placing tender kisses on one nipple and gently passing his thumb over the other. "It is my top priority to make each one of your secret desires come true." He moved over her, running his tongue across her chest to the other breast and encircling it in a slow and tormenting sweep. "Your wish is my command, *cara mia*."

She closed her eyes and the sun's bright light hallowed the insides of her lids. Losing herself in the warmth of his breath, the rapture of his touch, her body settled against his in a state of delight. Sapphy wanted to be nowhere else in the world but with Dante.

"Tell me, *cara*, what does this fantasy entail?"

"You and me." Sapphy saw the image clear in her mind and smiled. She'd fantasized about a moment like this many times when she was far away and alone at school. She'd fantasized about the same when she'd slept in her room down the hall from him as a teenager. Whether it was in the morning, at noon, or at night, making love to Dante was central to all her fantasies.

"You and I are here," he said in a deep voice.

She snuggled closer, looping her arms under his then over his shoulders. Keeping her eyes sealed tight, she scraped her teeth over her bottom lip.

"Fresh white sheets, the sun shining bright through the bellowing curtains, and the scent of the sea engulfing our bodies as we..."

She opened her eyes and looked up at him. She'd have referred to them as making love, but she needed assurance that he agreed.

Dante grinned. "I like the way your voice trails to a tiny whisper when your body reacts to me."

Adjusting her hips, he angled himself against her and gently entered her, filling a void only he could. His sexy gaze caressed her face as he marked her heart as his.

"Keep your eyes open, *tesoro mio*. I want to see every bit of ecstasy displayed in them," he breathed. "Please, allow me that pleasure."

Physically and emotionally, they moved together in harmony, climbing higher with each touch, stroke, and kiss. His body tensed and the pressure built as she held his gaze. He buried himself completely, and the pathos she'd felt for this man and had kept neatly contained for all these years was set free, diminishing any fears that were buried in her previous hesitation.

* * * *

It was noon when Sapphy stepped out of the shower. She tied the bathrobe snug about her waist. Wondering if the euphoria they'd shared had affected Dante the way it had her, she avoided making eye contact. She dreaded the possibility that it hadn't meant the same to him. Maybe it was just another night of sex.

"Would you like some coffee?" Dante asked, dressing in the large walk-in closet.

"Yes." She grabbed at the lame diversion to the emotions playing within her. Anything but facing rejection. "I'd love a cappuccino."

"*Daccordo.* I'll meet you on the terrace."

He strolled out in a pair of jeans, an unbuttoned blue and white striped shirt, and wet tousled hair. Everything about him was so handsome and yet so natural. Dante was all she could ask for in a man. The problem was all within her.

She'd lost everything she'd loved: her father, her mother, and the unborn sibling her mother had been carrying when she'd died. Fate wasn't kind to her. So, it was inevitable that she would end up losing Dante like she had the rest. And, this loss was guaranteed because of a stupid contract.

Regardless of his motivation for being with her, she would accept her fate and enjoy the little time she had with him. When he chose to move on, she would be mature and gracious. She owed him that simple courtesy. In the mean time, she would show any doubting acquaintance that her marriage was real.

Dressed in her own jeans and white button down shirt, she met Dante on the terrace. He stood and waited for her to sit before offering her a plate of fresh rolls and cheese.

She drank the dark, bitter coffee and was working on the crusty country bread when he reached for her hand.

"Let's go for a drive down to Positano," Dante suggested. "I can't think of a nicer place to be on a day like this. We could relax the afternoon away by the water and enjoy the fresh air. And if you're a real good girl and give me one of those lingering sweet kisses of yours, I might even have a surprise for you. What do you say?" There was a twinkle in his eyes, and his posture was totally relaxed. She liked him like that.

Closing her hand over his knuckles, she leaned forward and smoothed her tongue over his lips until they opened. Then, slowly, ever so gently, she explored the warmth of his mouth, enjoying his taste mingling with the sweetness of espresso he'd just finished. When a groan escaped his throat and she could feel him grinning, she ended the kiss.

"That is what I'm talking about," he said. "You can melt the polar ice caps with your lips."

Satisfied, she smiled and shrugged as the butterflies danced in her stomach. This time, for a good reason.

"You get the surprise." Dante pulled her onto his lap and nuzzled against the crook of her neck, trailing kisses from the sensitive part below her ear to her collarbone. "I enjoy having you like this."

"How's that?"

"To myself. No distractions." He cupped her face and feathered her cheek with his thumb. "Nobody else around. I have all your attention. Finally, after all this time, we are the way we're supposed to be."

Unable to digest his words, she swallowed hard and licked her lips.

"Don't go flaunting that tongue—unless you plan on using it," he teased in Italian.

"*Sì, seniore.*" Sapphy laughed and pulled herself off his lap. "In that case, a drive down the coast is fine by me."

"Good. Today, we enjoy the time alone the drive gives us. Tomorrow morning, we fly back to reality and work," he said, still holding her hand. "Get yourself a hat and pack a change of clothes."

"I have plenty of clothes in Positano," she protested.

"Just pack a change of clothes, *amore.*"

Her heart fluttered. She could get used to all of this. Sapphy cautioned herself to be careful, to remember that things rarely changed overnight and neither would their love affair.

Insecurities flooded Sapphy's psyche and the negative innuendoes of Carmella's conversation filled her mind. *I'm going to take things one moment at a time. And this very minute, he wants to be with me. That is all that counts. For now.*

Gazing at the man she loved, she knew she had no other option. She was going to make it work. She wanted it more than anything in the world, and it wasn't for the business benefit. But, regardless how hard she tried to avoid the subject, the earlier wakeup call nagged at her.

"Why did Carmella call here this morning?"

"Who knows? The woman is a control freak,"

Dante replied. "She wants to have her claws in every little detail of her daughter's life."

* * * *

Dante drove Sapphy's prized convertible and discussed plans for the week ahead. He was going to have a desk placed in his office for her. He wanted to work with her himself. With her talent and abilities, they would make a formidable team. They were going to create jobs for more of Naples's citizens and infuse the local economy with growth while taking the international industry by storm.

"I hate to tell you, but you already did that," Sapphy informed him. "Not that I won't try, but I don't think my influence will be as strong as you make it out to be."

"*Bella*, your influence is so much greater than you think." Dante placed his hand on her thigh and gave her a sideways grin. "Not only do you have Andreas Poulos's sharp business genes, but you are intelligent, beautiful, and powerful in your own right. Last night, you had the room buzzing with a simple appearance."

"That is because none of those people met *your* wife before," she said.

"Maybe," he conceded, cocking his head. "Imagine the effect you'll have when they see the rest of the real you. Amazing. There will be no stopping you."

"But what about the will? Our contract?" Sapphy had to know where she stood so that she could deal with it properly.

His jaw squared and the little muscle in the center of his cheek twitched. Gripping the steering wheel, he maneuvered the sports car on the curving road and did not reply. The rugged cliffs and the contrast of the serenity of the sea mirrored the expression on Dante's face. He was bothered, perhaps disappointed in her.

"We're adults," she continued. "We need to discuss things and set the foundation for our future."

"Not now," he said curtly. Down shifting into second gear, he slowed and took a right into a marina. He drove past many of the docked vessels to a large sailboat at the far end.

"Your surprise, *bambolina*," he said, indicating the impressive sailboat. "We're having lunch at our beach on the island."

Their beach. The one that they'd spend so much time at together before he'd left for school. That was the summer she'd fallen in love with him for real. Even though she was only thirteen when he'd gone away, it had been so much more than a crush or puppy love. She could never have admitted it, but it was then that she had made up her mind to marry Dante Morelli, simply not in the manner that she had. Not for duty and responsibility, but for love.

"Beautiful," she said, blinking back the tears. "I haven't been there in—"

"Ten years?" Dante asked, interrupting.

"Yes, ten years."

"Things change in ten years." He opened the door and unfolded his legs from behind the steering wheel. Walking around the car, he reached the passenger side and helped her out of the convertible. Dante held onto her hand and hooked it across his hips and into his back pocket. "Like you keep reminding me, we are no longer kids. We are adults now. So, we revisit our beach, and today, we make adult memories."

He snaked his arm around waist and pulled her against him, placing a kiss on her temple. "I've waited a long time for this, and I'm not waiting a minute longer."

Sapphy's heart hammered with joy. He hadn't

verbally answered her question, but his actions showed that he wanted her. Maybe even in the way that she wanted him. She nodded and relaxed against him, grateful for her good fortune, but weary that she was missing something.

She glanced toward the luxury sailboat fully equipped with the staff on deck, waiting for Dante and Sapphy to embark.

"Not quite the same mode of transportation we used back then," she said, admiring the beautiful vessel.

"Things do change in ten years." Dante chuckled and brushed his lips over her hair. "I want my hands free of sailing duties so that I could enjoy every minute with my wife. I want to feed her fresh berries as she sips on champagne, to hold her hair back from her lovely face as the wind whips through it, and to hug her tight against me for each and every moment I have with her on the water."

"Hm, sounds like you've planned out all the details of the afternoon." With a sense of unbelievable pleasure filling her chest, she flashed him a smile and gently touched his cheek. "What do you suggest I do?"

Grinning mischievously, he reached for her hand and rubbed her ring finger. "Decorate."

Wondering what he was implying, she glanced down at the simple gold band and then back up at his face. He couldn't possibly want her choosing curtain fabric for the cabins. As far as she knew, they didn't own this yacht. The SD yacht was a motorized monstrosity used for corporate events. Their personal vessels were small and cozy, right for individual excursions. She didn't know anything about a yacht like this.

"Don't be so serious, *bambolina*," Dante said,

slipping a ring over her finger. "Now that you're in Naples and truly with me, I thought we should personalize a few of the things close to our hearts and daily lives. Your jewelry is a small start. You need one of these," he added, raising her hand so that the magnificent diamond reflected the sunlight.

"Oh my God!" She moved her fingers and the ring sparkled. The setting matched her simple gold band, but the diamond was breathtaking. Cut into a perfect round solitaire, the precious stone spanned the width of her finger and dazzled the sun's rays into a perfect rainbow. "It's stunning."

"Not half as stunning as the woman who wears it," he replied, not taking his gaze off of her. "The look on your face makes it all the more precious. I am guessing you like it."

"You're guessing correctly," she said, admiring the ring. "But it isn't necessary. You didn't have to do this."

"I did not have to do it." Dante gathered her into his embrace and kissed her mouth. "I wanted to. I never gave you a proper ring when we married. It is long overdue, but at least I have the pleasure of doing it now."

Sapphy stared at the rock on her finger. It could only mean one thing: He felt the same as she did.

"I love it, Dante." Happy beyond her dreams, she jumped into his embrace and wrapped her arms around his neck. "Thank you."

Scooping her into his hold, he secured his grip under her knees and settled her against his chest as he carried her onboard the boat. "Then, we are good," he whispered to her.

The captain greeted them, and Dante requested they set sail immediately. Making his way to the open deck, Dante sat on a plush couch, keeping her on his lap. She snuggled against him and let the wind pick up her hair as they headed into the bay.

"Would you like a drink?" Dante asked as the staff uncorked a bottle of champagne.

She shook her head. "I just want to sit here and take in the view."

"I thought seasickness no longer affected you. Is your stomach queasy?"

"No." Sapphy laughed, remembering how her love of the water was born. "I want to enjoy your arms around me. That's all."

The sailboat cut across the tiny waves and arrived at their beach in less than a quarter of the time it used to take them when they sailed out to the island alone.

There was an elegant picnic waiting for them on a desolate part of the beach. A large canvas tent was set on the southern edge of the sand by a tall cliff they used to dive off of. The clear blue water lapped at the shore only feet from the table adorned with skewers of grilled vegetables, succulent seafood, and fresh fruit. There was a carafe of Chianti in the center of the table with two wine glasses on either side.

"This is very romantic," Sapphy said, swaying to the soft music mingling with the sound of the surf. "When did you have a chance to arrange for all of it?"

"Trade secret," Dante replied, pulling out her chair so she could sit. "I thought that since things change so much with time, you might enjoy a feast at a table, rather than a sandwich on the sand."

"Oh, I don't know." Life couldn't get better than this. Sapphy was flying high on the day's euphoria. "The table might be good to eat at, but the sand could serve a different purpose rather nicely."

"Duly noted, *amore mia*." Dante held her hand as he rounded the table and took his seat. "The sand does have interesting possibilities." He raised her hand to his lips and his eyes promised her much more on their private beach.

Being with Dante in this manner was surreal. They chatted about old times as the staff prepared the pasta course, served the skewered meat, refreshed the wine, then promptly disappeared.

Sapphy and Dante drank, ate, and made love beneath the shelter of the tent for hours. When the sheen of their fervor for each other glistened on their bodies, and the breeze was cool on their heated skin, he held her tight while her breathing returned to normal.

"*Cara mia*, the sun is setting." Dante kissed her nose, her eyelids, her forehead, and at last, her mouth. Releasing her lips, he caressed her hair back from her face. "Either we sleep on the boat tonight, or we sail to the mainland soon."

"Mainland," she replied, standing and pulling the light spread up with her. "However, I do think I'll need my clothes before we go."

He laughed and tossed her a pair of lace panties. They showered and changed onboard while the yacht sailed back to the dock. Then they drove the twenty minutes to Sant'Anna in quiet comfort.

* * * *

Arriving at Sant'Anna, Sapphy felt Dante tense and his lighthearted mood dissipate. A pit, heavy like a ball of raw dough, settled in the center of her stomach as Gabriella greeted them and latched on to Dante's neck.

It didn't sit well with Sapphy that Gabriella clung to Dante like there was no shame in the act, and the splendor of the afternoon evaporated with every word the other woman whispered in the intimate embrace.

Carmella met them in the foyer and pulled Sapphy to the side and away from Dante.

"So, you have finally decided that family responsibilities have a place in your life and you have returned to Italy." The snide remark was compounded by the disapproving twist on the older woman's lips. "Things don't change just because you will them to."

Dante cleared his throat, and Carmella extended her arms to him, as if in sympathy. He shot Carmella a chilling look of warning and made no effort to embrace her.

"I suggest you amend your tone toward my wife. Or else, you are free to direct your comments to me."

"You misunderstand." Carmella dropped her hands and took a step back. "I have no qualms with you, Dante. You're very diligent in assuring that things are in order, and I certainly didn't mean to imply that you did anything out of line."

"What did you mean, Carmella?"

"Your actions were out of character this morning," Carmella said in a low whisper, as if she hoped he wouldn't hear.

Dante crossed his arms over his chest and remained silent, but his flaming glare more that spoke his discontent.

"I must admit that it distressed me when you did not return home after I called you." Assuming a matronly stance, Carmella looked from Dante to Sapphy and back again. "I was so worried. My blood pressure went very high until my daughter called."

"But she did call, and Gabriella informed you that she was fine and would be back at Santa Anna to pack for her trip." Dante upturned his palm in annoyance. "Why would you think that anything was wrong? And, what does my wife have to do with it?"

"I didn't say your wife was to blame," Carmella replied.

Sapphy held her breath as Dante made it clear that Carmella had no right to consider anything about his wife, question his motives or to keep tabs on him.

Gabriella's fingers skimmed her throat in a nervous tapping, and Sapphy felt sorry for her. The poor woman shifted her weight from one foot to the other, seemingly searching for the strength to speak. But she didn't. Gabriella's eyes grew big and her throat was covered in red streaks as her mother refused to apologize about overreacting and creating such a fuss.

"*Ciccia*, there is no reason to be upset." Dante moved to stand between mother and daughter. "Please join me and Sapphy on the terrace for a drink, and we'll chat about the week."

Giving Sapphy a meek smile, Gabriella nodded. This was not the confident and capable, even bitchy at times, woman that Sapphy had associated with Gabriella.

Taking Sapphy's hand, Dante whispered in her ear. "Don't look so concerned. This is typical Carmella happenings."

Smiling, he closed his fingers over hers and brushed his thumb pad over her knuckles. Sapphy did not miss Carmella's quick glance at the intimate gesture and the frown that followed.

"Yes, Gabriella," Sapphy added, emphasizing the name so that it was clear that the invitation was an exclusive one. "Please join us on the veranda."

"Thank you." Gabriella's gaze skirted to Dante. "Let me go change, and I'll meet you out there."

Gabriella vanished up the stairs, and without another word to Carmella, Dante led Sapphy to the terrace.

"The woman is a nuisance," he said, tickling Sapphy's back with his fingers as he placed a silk wrap on her shoulders.

"I feel horrible for Gabriella," Sapphy confessed. "I've never seen her like that before."

"You have never really gotten to know the woman Gabriella has turned into," he said. "I believe you would like her if you gave her a chance and did not associate mother and daughter as one."

It wasn't so much the mother-daughter association that bothered her. It was Gabriella's constant involvement with Dante that nagged at her. His stepsister was constantly with him and very protective of their relationship. Gabriella had attempted to minimize Sapphy's communication with Dante on more than one occasion.

"True, I'm not familiar with Gabriella, but I am also not blind." Sapphy tugged the shawl over her shoulders to ward off the chill in the night air. "At the risk of sounding possessive and jealous, she is always at your side and seems to turn to you for everything."

"No, *cara mia*. Not everything," Dante cautioned. "Gabriella and I do have an excellent relationship, but we are friends, good friends, the way siblings should be. There is nothing more. Don't let your imagination, or Carmella, convince you otherwise."

"She works with you and takes care of all your needs."

"I can't tell you how flattered I am that it concerns you. I'm glad you care." Dante grinned, but shook his head. "Gabriella has only been at the office this week. My assistant took time to spend with her mother, and Gabriella needed an excuse to get away from Carmella. Come to think of it, we use headquarters as a continuous escape from Carmella."

She wanted to believe him, wanted to take what he said as gospel, but Sapphy was having a difficult time. "Why am I informed that she is at work with you every time I call?"

"Informed? By Carmella?" He chuckled and raised his shoulders. "Obviously, Carmella is disillusioned about the possible relationship Gabriella and I could have—if you were out of the picture. I would not put it past the wicked woman to try to push you away. Maybe the fortune my father left her isn't enough. Maybe she wants access to our money via her daughter."

What a shame for Marco Morelli to have spent his final years with a woman that was only interested in his wallet, and how peculiar that Sapphy's marriage with his son was orchestrated to avoid that type of scenario.

"Apparently, the old woman has alienated her flesh and blood so much that Gabriella doesn't share anything with her mother." Dante raised his glass and swirled his wine. "I don't believe Gabriella has even told her that she is an in-demand model in Milano."

"Gabriella is a successful model?"

"Oh, yes." Dante nodded and took a drink. "She is very successful. The man she was with last night is an American producer who approached her to be the spoke person for his documentary. It concerns me a little because I haven't heard anything about him. He's appeared out of nowhere. I can't force her, but I've suggested she pass on the documentary."

"Is she going to do it?"

"I think so," he replied. "Much like you, Gabriella is extremely stubborn and proud. She is confident that her instincts are correct about this man. She has specifically requested that I stay out of her business and not even investigate his background."

Sapphy rubbed her arm, not only for warmth, but for lack of something to do. She didn't know how to respond. She wasn't sure how to feel about his disclosures on Gabriella.

The information was too much for a woman to absorb in one day. All she had believed was jumbled in a ball of myth and truth. Taking a deep breath, she closed her eyes and chose to trust the man who held her heart. After all, trust is a choice when the other person deserves it, and Dante had earned it.

Gabriella arrived and the conversation eventually turned to the London meeting, scheduled for the following morning. Sapphy excused herself. "It's been a long day, so I'll let you make plans for the trip."

* * * *

Wrapped in a towel, Sapphy applied lotion to her legs. She was almost done when there was a knock at the bathroom door. Securing the knot, she cracked the door and peeked out.

"You growing shy with me?" Dante grinned, stepping into the pink bathroom and pulling her into his embrace. "It's a little late for that, *bambolina*."

"No, not shy," she whispered against his shoulder.

"Then what?"

"It's late." She moved out of his hold and back to the mirror. "Don't you need to pack for your trip?"

"No." He pressed up behind her and wrapped his arms around her middle. "The London meeting doesn't warrant an overnight stay. I'll be back late in the evening. Will you wait up for me?" Peppering her neck with kisses, he slipped his hand inside the towel and cupped her breast.

Leaning her head back on his shoulder, she closed her eyes and let the intimate caress smooth away her worries. "I'll wait."

The towel dropped to the floor and he turned her to face him. "I can shower here if you want, but I think I will look scary tiptoeing naked across the hall. How about we meet in the room with the larger bed from now on? Our bedroom."

Pleasure and relief ricocheted through her body. *Our bedroom.* Nodding her head, she exhaled and told him to go ahead. "Let me get ready and collect my things for the morning."

Claiming her mouth, he swept the lingering flavor of the limoncello over her lips before releasing her. "I'll try to be patient." He picked up the towel and secured it about her. "But, don't take long. Or else, I'll storm in here naked and throw you over my shoulder to carry you across the hall."

Chapter Seven

"That is preposterous." Dante said into his cellular. "It is the middle of the night."

Sapphy forced her eyes open and stared at the darkness. The clock on the nightstand glowed four-thirty-three, and other than Dante's low voice, there was no noise in the house.

Pushing off the covers, Dante sat on the edge of the bed and turned his back to her. His shoulders, outlined by the dim moonlight streaming in from the window, hunkered over the phone.

"When did we learn of this?" He raked his fingers through his hair and nodded while the caller spoke. "Are you sure that the source could be trusted?"

Sapphy sat up and touched his back. "Is everything all right?" she whispered.

Swinging his arm behind him, he caressed her thigh and encouraged her to go back to sleep. Sapphy didn't lie down. She scooted closer and rested her chin in his shoulder.

"*Daccordo*. I'll be in by six. I'll meet you in the office." Dante snapped the phone shut and turned to her. "Go back to bed, *cara*. I'll send the helicopter for you at eight."

"You're going to the office now?"

"Sorry, Sapphy, but I need to go in as soon as possible." Dante stood and walked towards the en-suite bath. "Antonio has arranged an early meeting. I want to make sure everything is in order before we begin."

"What is so important that it can't wait a little for you to sleep like a normal person?"

"Petos."

She must have misheard. As far as Sapphy knew, Dante had instructed Antonio to find a different solution; one that didn't involve the Greek-American. And unless he was going to reconsider the sale of her father's land, there was no reason for Dante to speak with Petos.

Switching on the bedside light, she threw back the covers and followed him to the bathroom. "Dante, I will not let you sell the land on Zakynthos."

"I won't." Loading his toothbrush with paste, he let out a long breath and shook his head. "I don't understand why you want to hold onto that property so bad, but I hope that one day you will let me in on the secret. Your fellow Greek is very adamant about acquiring the land. He continues to make outrages offers, and he insists that he needs to meet with *you* personally."

"I don't want to sell it. I can't," she said, stepping into the shower stall. "I'll be ready in a few minutes. Don't go without me." She wasn't about to stay behind. If the meeting involved the Zakynthos property, she was going to be there. Then his words sank in. "Me? He insists on meeting with me?"

Sapphy shivered under the steady stream of water beating on her skin, and the chills filling her body had nothing to do with the water temperature. Dante's eyes had gone blank, his demeanor was cold, and the damn phone call seemed to be at the root of these changes.

Yesterday, Dante may have acted like he wanted her as his wife, but it was Sapphy who had interpreted his actions. He never said he loved her, or that he wanted to cancel their marriage contract and the divorce. How could she assume what his actions meant and trust blindly his intentions?

It was her pride that kept her from explaining her reasons for not selling the land. The only thing it'd accomplish was to establish herself as a wimp, who would lose all control of the situation. Dante would do what was expected of him and take care of everything. He always did, but whether he did it out of obligation or love, she wouldn't have a say in how things were handled. Sapphy didn't want that. She needed to do this on her own, of her own abilities, and without relinquishing the last bit of her father's trust.

Reuniting with her aunt was a family matter that her father would want done with dignity and minimum disturbance to his sister's life. Her father had doubted that Thea Eleni would even remember being adopted and taken away from her brother and off the island.

Knocking on the glass door, Dante told her he'd wait downstairs and disappeared. He hadn't bothered to join her in the shower. He had barely spoken to her.

* * * *

Exactly ten minutes later, she rushed down the stairs with a jacket strewn over her arm. It was still dark outside, but there was a light in the kitchen, and the heavenly smell of fresh espresso drew her into the cozy room off the dining hall.

Therese placed a cup in front of Dante, and then smiled up at Sapphy. "*Buongiorno, dolcezza.*"

"*Buongiorno, Therese.* You shouldn't have woken

up so early," Sapphy said, kissing the matronly woman's cheek.

"Ah, I like to see my boy off when he is home." Therese rubbed the back of Dante's neck as if he was five years old. "And now that my girl is here, too, I wouldn't miss it for the world." Giving Sapphy a wink, Therese patted the chair beside Dante and placed a second cup of coffee on the table. "A morning like this should be celebrated."

Heat rose to Sapphy's face. Suddenly, she felt like a kid herself—like she'd been caught kissing a boy by the front door when she wasn't allowed to see him.

Ridiculous, Dante is my husband, and I shouldn't feel guilty about getting out of his bed at this horrific hour. No blushing!

"Seeing you in the morning always makes my day go right," Sapphy confessed. "I'm glad you're up."

Therese had been with Dante since Sapphy could remember, but she was so much more than an employee. She was like the aunt who kept the family and household running smooth when things were hectic. There was genuine concern and love in the relationship.

Swallowing the buttered bread, Dante smiled at Therese.

"Not to mention that she makes the best coffee in all of Italy. Especially, on short notice. How you knew that we needed you this early amazes me." He dropped his napkin beside the plate, stood, placed a loud kiss on Therese's cheek, and nodded to Sapphy. "*Andiamo.* The helicopter is waiting."

Saying a quick goodbye to Therese, Sapphy hurried to the private landing pad off the west side of the house.

The whirling blades picked up the earth and made

a thunderous noise as Dante took her hand and guided her through the mayhem. She preferred to drive, but there was no time, and the helicopter was Dante's primary choice of transportation.

Seated in the cabin, she glanced back at Santa Anna and noticed a curtain drop shut on the third floor. Carmela was watching them. The woman has devious and backhanded. Sapphy never understood what Marco Morelli saw in her.

"Don't we need to wait for Gabriella?" Sapphy called over the raucous.

"No. I don't need an assistant for the meeting. Like I said last night, Gabriella's involvement in the trip was orchestrated to get her away from Carmella. She will find some excuse and leave at a decent hour."

Suddenly, Sapphy felt sorry for Gabriella. How terrible to need an excuse to escape your mother. How miserable to have to avoid the person that is supposed to love you unconditionally. A mother should treasure and be treasured.

Sad.

The bubble-topped machine ascended into the sky and Sapphy welcomed the darkness as it engulfed her in the steely silence the headset provided. She wanted to ask Dante about the conference call, but her husband appeared preoccupied, even annoyed. The dark stubble on his jaw, which only an hour ago was amazingly sexy, now gave him an intimidating aura and placed him behind a wall and far from her.

Or maybe, the drama was in Sapphy's head. She was stuck between logic and emotion and didn't know which way to turn. Her father would never object to her asking for Dante's help, but her pride did. She'd depended on him for too long and for everything. The only things she'd accomplished on her own were her studies. In this instance, she had to be self-sufficient.

Sapphy had the means to locate her aunt. She had the maturity and confidence to approach her long lost relative. It was a possibility well within her reach to do. She would do it and silence Petos' requests.

On the other hand, confiding her needs to Dante would make the task so much simpler. However, in doing so, she opened herself to a possible hurt. And even harder, she had to make a choice and place her trust in *his* hands. It would be a conscious decision, not a result of circumstance or coincidence.

Her thoughts spun as fast as the helicopter's blades with the varying choices available to her. She wasn't feeling capable or confident, but she, like the helicopter, had to land at some point.

Stoic and rigid, Dante stared past the front window and didn't speak to her. He didn't reach for her or give her a sideways glance. He, too, seemed to require the mental solitude she'd been absorbed in. Eventually, she reached for him and slid her hand beneath his, setting it on his lap. Being alone - together- seemed best. She took a deep breath and closed her eyes. Once Dante squeezed her hand, she exhaled and her body relaxed.

Neither of them spoke until they touched down.

"You don't need to be here," Dante said unbuckling her restraints. "I can take care of him on my own."

"I know you can," she replied with a smile. "But, I want to be here. I don't want you to handle this for me."

His forehead wrinkled and he shook his head. Helping Sapphy out of the chopper, Dante instructed the pilot on the day's events. She gathered her briefcase against her chest and waited for him to unlock the building's roof entrance as the chopper took flight again. A pale light glowed on the eastern horizon and announced the arrival of dawn. Soon, the sun would rise and the workday would be underway.

Stepping through the heavy metal door into the sterile space, he placed a palm on the small of her back and guided her through the maze. The area was not the penthouse floor, but a small fireproof annex used for storage of files. Since the first time she'd been up there, Sapphy was certain a person could get lost in the aisles stacked over two meters high with metal boxes.

Dante punched in a code on the keypad beside the executive lift, and with an additional voice command, the elevator descended to the floor with his office.

"I was unaware of your personal relationship with Petos," Dante said, spitting out an accusation and looking at her in disbelief and disappointment before turning his back. He wiped at a fingerprint on the steel door.

"I don't have a personal relationship with him," she protested.

The elevator stopped and he stepped aside, allowing her to exit ahead of him. Perturbed with his insinuation, she second-guessed her recent decision of explaining her position to him.

The lights turned on automatically as they progressed down the empty hallway to his office. There was no reason for any of the employees to be in the office at dawn, and the cleaning crew finished at midnight, so the building was extremely quiet. Sapphy's insides shuddered with the sound of his breathing.

How stupid! Grow up and tell him to be rational.

"When I am dealing with business acquaintances and don't have all the facts, I am at a great disadvantage. I especially do not like being put in that position by you, Sapphyra." Sliding his briefcase atop the desk, he cleared his throat as if he choked on the resentment. "Is there anything else you would care to tell me before Antonio arrives with your *friend*?"

She didn't appreciate his renewed condescending tone, but it wasn't the appropriate time to play games. Petos was coming to the office, and her priority was to settle this nonsense and keep the suspect man away from the Zakynthos estate.

Sapphy placed her own case on the conference table. Noting that the large rectangular table had been replaced by a square one with two seats on each side, she wondered if the arrangement was an intentional display of joint leadership or a coincidence.

"You and I will sit with our backs to the window," he said.

Damn. She hated that he could address her questions before she had an opportunity to ask them.

"Andreas Petos strolled into the Student Union one day when I was recouping after a killer final," she offered. "He introduced himself in a nice and polite manner, and we talked over a cup of coffee for about an hour about Greece and our childhood summers on the wonderful beaches of the country we both love. That was the extent of our interaction. Is that what you consider a relationship?"

She sat in the chair and crossed her arms over her chest. The idea of her hiding a secret relationship with Petos was ridiculous—let alone the allegation that she'd withheld any important business information from Dante.

He remained standing and leaned against the table, meeting her gaze. His dark eyes were intense, but lacked any sparkle. Flat and accusing, they pierced through her confidence and made her feel like she was testifying in a witness box.

"Did he have flowers delivered to your apartment that night?" Dante paced the area and swiftly turned on his heels to stare at her as if he'd proven that she'd committed the crime. "Did he ask you to dinner?"

"No," she said, curling her fingers into a tight fist. "He invited me to lunch." She stood from her seat and walked around the table to face him. Dante was out of line, and she refused to be talked to in that manner, yet again.

The muscle in the center of his cheek twitched, but his jaw squared and he didn't respond. Stuffing his hands in his pockets, he rolled his lips together in distaste and stared.

"It isn't a felony to receive a bouquet of fresh flowers from someone, so stop acting like it is." She wasn't going to let his wronged suggestions slide. She'd done nothing to be ashamed of. "And, you have no right to be possessive or jealous of any previous relationship—even if it is only in your head. We had agreed to live our personal lives as single people. Remember?"

Dante nodded and looked away.

The sun crept over the horizon and painted the sky with a glowing orange hue. The security system announced Antonio's arrival, which meant Petos would be upstairs in less than seven minutes. She needed to get herself together before that.

"Did, or do, you have a personal relationship with Petos?" Dante repeated in a strained and monotone voice.

"No." She shook her head. Dante had never acted like this before and it wasn't a side of him she liked. Blowing out a breath, she moved back to her seat, opening and closing her fist to relieve the numbness from her nails digging into her palm.

"I believe you," he said in a low voice.

"Oh, how gracious of the Great Dante." She threw her hands up at the side of her head and pretended to bow. "I don't see what the big deal is, or why you should be questioning me."

"Because..." His gaze dropped to the floor as his voice trailed. He didn't finish his answer.

Vulnerable. Dante appeared vulnerable. His broad shoulders drew close and his chest barely rose as he breathed. He slowly came around the table and stood beside her.

Regaining her composure, she reached for his hand and looked up at him. "I don't think—"

He placed his finger on her lips as the elevator dinged its arrival. "Later, *cara mia*."

In a flash, he sat beside her, his body relaxed and casually turned towards her as if they were lounging lazily on a typical morning. Putting on the appropriate airs for the necessary appearance, he was back in control.

"Good morning, Mr. Morelli," Antonio called, still out of view. "Mr. Petos and I have arrived." He knocked on the doorframe and appeared at the entrance. "Mrs. Morelli." Stepping into the room, he smiled at Sapphy and introduced Andreas Petos.

Petos followed Antonio into the room, and Dante's face hardened while his grip on her hand tightened. He rose and extended his other hand to both men. "Morning, gentlemen. Welcome to SD Holdings, Mr. Petos."

"Please call me Andreas." The atmosphere, thick and heavy, sparked with distrust between the two handsome men as Petos accepted Dante's hand.

"Thank you for seeing me at such a time. Antonio explained that your schedule is very difficult today, and I'm grateful for not having to postpone my flight back to the States."

When the Greek-American turned his gaze on her, Sapphy coughed out of surprise. During their previous meeting, she hadn't noticed how good-looking Petos was. He was tall and stood broad shoulder to broad shoulder with Dante. His dark hair was styled short above his collar and was peppered with a touch of grey at the temples that accentuated the sculpted angles of his face. But it was his dazzling blue eyes that captivated her attention. They had an unreadable agenda that intrigued her most.

"Sapphyra, it is a pleasure to see you again." Petos nodded and took her left hand in his, a much too casual and intimate greeting. The left hand was, as her father used to say, the hand of the heart.

With a low, but unmistakable hiss, Dante gestured for Andreas have a seat. Antonio sat to Dante's right and placed a voice recorder and legal pad on the table.

"Not to be rude, but since we're limited on time, let us start," Dante said. "You must have a pressing reason for wanting to meet on such short notice."

Andreas glanced at the recorder and shook his head. "This is not a professional matter. I'm here on a personal level."

Waving his hand, Dante indicated for Antonio to remove the device. Tension settled over the meeting like morning fog, making the expansive office suite claustrophobic. The two men locked gazes like two wolves from rival packs protecting their turf. Uneasiness traveled up and down Sapphy's spine.

Dante was a master at fostering the proper appearance to gain the upper hand, and his body relaxed against his leather seat as he pulled Sapphy's hand onto his knee. Only the way his thumb pushed against the inside of her wrist signaled that he was not as comfortable as he seemed.

She looked around the table and wondered who would cave first and initiate a real discussion. Neither one of the men seemed inclined to lower his battle arms and reveal the true purpose for the early morning gathering. Petos was on the edge of his seat, leaning forward as if anxious to begin, but he seemed to be waiting for something. Dante didn't invite him to proceed and blocked any avenue for the other man to feel comfortable. Antonio, sitting between them, kept the legal pad displayed on the table and a pen clutched in his hand.

"Mr. Petos, you are aware that we will not entertain the possibility of selling the land on Zakynthos to you," Sapphy began, seeing no alternative to the standoff. "That was an internal—temporary—misunderstanding because we were out of communication for that brief period of time. In other words, I'm afraid you may be disappointed today."

The brightness faded from the deepest blue eyes she'd ever seen. Andreas cleared his throat and intertwined his fingers on the table as he nodded.

"The reason I requested to meet with you was because I couldn't gain access to Sapphyra if I didn't," Petos said to Dante. "In truth, my business is with her and doesn't concern your company in the least. Is it possible that I speak with Sapphyra privately?"

The crimson flush on Dante's neck betrayed his supposed cool composure. Sapphy's heart skipped a beat as he gripped the edge of the table and his fingertips turned white.

"Anything that concerns my wife, concerns me,"

Dante bit out.

The dense fog grew suffocating. She had to make a conscious effort to fill her lungs. Pulling her hand from his knee, she wiped her palms on her skirt, and then placed, what she hoped was, a reassuring hand on Dante's arm.

"That's okay," she said, a plea to avoid a confrontation filling her tone. "I don't mind. If my input can be of any assistance to Mr. Petos, I will be happy to talk with him."

Resting his arms on the table, Petos flashed an appreciative grin.

"This meeting is over." Dante rose to his feet and glared at the other man. "There is no reason for further conversation. My wife has made it clear that the land is not for sale- regardless of the price. So, don't waste your time."

"I respect and understand your position, Mr. Morelli." Petos hesitated, but he did not stand to leave. "On my honor, I am not here to manipulate Sapphyra."

Sapphy pulled on Dante's forearm, urging him to take his seat. Petos's tone was sincere and she didn't feel threatened. Rather, the familiar creasing at the corners of his eyes when he spoke with such grave concern encouraged her to ask him to continue. She had to know what business this stranger had with her.

"Mr. Petos, my husband and I keep no secrets from each other. Not personal. Not professional." In an apparent display of unity, she feathered her fingers over Dante's and then intertwined them. "Please, tell us what concern brings us together today."

Petos's intense Mediterranean-blue gaze skidded toward Antonio in apprehension. Clearly, he didn't want an audience.

She cleared her throat, anticipating the answer

before asking the question, and turned to Antonio. "Would you mind terribly if I asked you to check if the staff has arrived? It is way too early for my brain to function smoothly, and I could certainly use some coffee if she has."

She swiped at the invisible haze and laughed a little too forced, but the attorney accepted the exit queue and left the three of them alone.

"Most likely, you are both familiar with what I need to discuss," Petos said. "However, I'm sure it is from a different perspective." Petos couldn't hide his discomfort. Repositioning his hands, he scraped perfect white teeth over his bottom lip.

"This is difficult for me, because I don't want you to think that I say this with any aggression or with personal entitlement, but I have an obligation to my grandmother. She is getting older and has not asked anything from me but this one thing. To find her brother."

He looked directly at Sapphy, and sparks danced under her skin. Inhaling deep, she shook her head and ignored the tingling the goose bumps on her arms.

"It is true, Sapphyra." Andreas nodded. "Please let me relay my story for you."

She tightened her hold on Dante's hand.

"When my grandmother was very young, she'd wake from her sleep, screaming every night. Her parents would hold her in their arms until she would fall asleep. It wasn't until she was a teenager that she was able to sleep through the night, but she never forgot.

"In this nightmare, *yiayia* was extremely young. She was alone, playing with a doll, when the smoke crept up the tiny staircase to the room she shared with an older brother. She yelled and screamed, calling for her mother, but there was no answer. She saw the flames reaching from the window below her, but thank God, her young mind understood enough not to run to the fire.

"Clutching the rag doll, she dropped to the floor between the two cots in the tiny room and cried as her beloved home smoldered beneath her. Soon, the smoke made it impossible to see, and she closed her eyes and prayed."

Sapphy wiped the moisture from the corner of her eye. She knew the story. She knew of the terror the fire and smoke inflicted. She also knew the pain revisiting the small home caused her father because of the loss of his parents and the disappearance of his sister.

"She envisioned Jesus spreading his arms wide and calling her into His embrace. Then, she heard him, and thought that her brother had died and had returned to guide her into God's light. Her brother lifted her off the floor, and she hid her face against his shoulder, thankful that he had come back for her. He'd come to help her.

"He carried her and kissed her forehead, all the while whispering how much he would always love her. With unbelievable strength for a young, scrawny boy, he hoisted her outside the window, told her not to be frightened, and dropped her."

Sapphy's hand flew to her mouth and smothered her gasp. She couldn't hold back the sobs. It couldn't be the same story. No. Petos's grandmother couldn't have escaped the drop without injury. According to her father, her aunt had no injuries.

"She thought it was her way to heaven, and then a bony body met hers and a pair of arms wrapped around her. A young boy yelled something she didn't understand and stood her on her feet. He ran to the front door and continued to holler at the top of his lungs."

Petos stopped speaking.

Dante pulled her into his arms and pushed her hair away from her face, cradling her against his chest. His warm breath caressed her skin, as his arms held her heart together, oblivious to the professional image they'd initially required for the meeting..

"Do not cry, *cara*," Dante whispered. "They all made it out alive. They survived." He rocked her gently and held her tight. "Let's take a break, my friend."

"No, no," she said, running the back of her hand across her cheeks. She looked at Petos and into a mirror of her own eyes. The same color and shape as her father's. Eyes belonging to a man who had her father's name: Andreas.

"Marco Morelli placed your grandmother on her feet and then ran to the door and yelled for his friend to follow his voice out of the smoke filled house." Sapphy insisted on finishing the story. She had to be sure.

"Three Nazi soldiers showed up. They were not friendly and barked at the girl." Andreas flattened his palm on the table and swept it from side to side. "A woman appeared and took the little girl's hand, claiming her daughter had strayed from their home in the village. She pulled her away from the house as her brother and the other boy ran to hide in the olive grove. The little girl was the only one who knew the boys were there. She waived at them, and that was the last she time she saw them."

Sapphy held tight to Dante's arm and stared at the man sitting across the table. There was no doubt.

Silence.

The sunlight streamed through the window and

illuminated the large space of the room. Warmth flooded the area and gave her the courage to leave Dante's side.

Sapphy slowly walked around the table, and Petos stood.

"*Yiayia* Eleni was three," she whispered.

"I found you." Petos laughed with relief and gathered Sapphy into his arms. "I knew the moment I saw you in the Union that you were the one." He crushed her against his muscular chest and kissed the top of her head. "There is no mistaking your eyes."

He kept his arms around her for a long time, as she buried her face into his shirt and drenched it with tears of happiness.

Dante stood guard over the exchange. He knew the story, but he wasn't going to take Petos at his word without verification. True, there was no denying the strong physical resemblance between Sapphy and Petos, but his wife was a public figure and her picture was easy to come by. If someone wished to weasel his way into her life through physical similarities, he could do it with careful planning and work.

Petos was shrewd and cunning. Approximately ten years Dante's senior, Andreas Petos was well on his way to building his own empire from a very small start. Dante didn't know enough about him to trust the man. Why had Petos attempted to buy the Zantè property and not presented himself as a family member? Did he have an ulterior motive?

In fairness, Dante didn't know enough about Petos to dismiss him either. He shifted his weight and crossed his arms over his chest. He had work to do in order to verify the man's identity and understand his motives.

"I learned of our families' connection a few months ago. My grandmother discovered she was adopted recently, and wasn't sure how to go about finding her relatives. You see, there aren't records, but we know her adoptive parents were very young at the time. We think that my great-grandmother was only fourteen or fifteen when she lied about her age and left the island. She told the family as much once my great-grandfather died last Christmas. For all those years, *yiayia* believed her memory was only a dream." Petos said, wiping the tears from Sapphy's cheeks. "I'm sorry I missed meeting your father."

"So, where do we go from here?" Sapphy asked.

Petos's answer would give Dante a better feel for the man. He eagerly awaited the response.

"I have two things to request," Petos said.

The hair on the back of Dante's neck prickled. He'd just met her, and he had things to request. Not a good sign.

"Anything," Sapphy replied.

Dante hastily moved to her side and placed an arm around her. There was no way Sapphy was going to be taken advantage of. Even by family.

"Hold on. Sapphyra. Let's get to know Andreas," Dante said, meeting her gaze and pleading with her to slow down.

"That is the core of my first request," Andreas stated with ease. "Please allow me the time to return home, tell my grandmother about you, and organize a get-together. She will be so eager to meet you."

"I would like that very much." Sapphy smiled and gave a slight hop as she clasped her hands together at her chest. She was happy. "Would you like us to come to the States, or can she travel?"

"She is healthy. She can travel, but perhaps it

would be faster if you were able to visit her in New York the initial time. Obviously, you are both welcome to stay with me."

"We have a home in New York," Dante said. "Thank you for the invitation."

"When can we go?" Sapphy looked up at him, and Dante was stunned by the anticipation in her face.

"I wish we could have met sooner, but after I had verified all the available information and I tried to reach you in New York, I was told that you had come to Naples." Andreas's disappointment was evident in the sadness of his gaze. "I followed as soon as I could, but it was like Fort Knox over here. Sapphyra, you are the precious gold. It was impossible to reach you directly without jumping through massive hoops. That is a good thing."

Andreas turned to Dante. "I owe you so much. I've learned that your father was the other boy at the burning house. He saved my grandmother and her brother. Today, you are by our Sapphyra's side, taking care of her and seeing to all her needs. Please accept my deepest gratitude for all you have done for my family."

"Sapphyra is *my* family, and therefore, *my* responsibility. I have not done anything that any man would not do for his family." Dante projected his voice strongly and drew Sapphy's gaze to his. "Your cousin is my wife and the woman I love."

Chapter Eight

Tapping her pen on the blotter, Sapphy gazed dreamily out the large window. He'd said she was the woman he loved. She'd believed it. *That* couldn't have been for show.

He loved her.

His wife.

Dante loved Sapphy.

She leaned back on the headrest and tapped her toes on the floor in a little song of pleasure. Twirling the big executive chair, she threw a triumphant fist in the air. All morning she'd been afraid to breathe, lest she bust the bliss bubble she'd been encased in since the words had left Dante's lips.

"I'm loved. I'm a niece, and I'm a cousin," she said to herself. "Could things get any better?"

No. Things were perfect.

Petos wasn't the bad guy, but he was family and had brought her to *baba's* baby sister. She was learning the ropes of the business in the best possible way. And, most importantly, Dante loved her.

Everything about the day had been magnificent. She was happy, liked being a part of SD, and loved her husband. No more secrets. Sapphy'd let him know how lucky she felt and how much she loved *him* as soon as he returned from London.

Since Dante's office was the size of an expansive suite, space wasn't an issue when he'd insisted she be set up in it. The staff had arranged her desk and computer against the wall opposite his, and there was still enough room for a smaller conference table and the sitting area and wet bar looking out over the Bay. In all honesty, the view she craved most, was Dante seated across from her the majority of the workday.

"Well, that's tomorrow. Tomorrow will be the first day of the rest of my life, and I will live it exactly as I want. It is a fairytale come true."

Smiling, she turned her focus to the ECL portfolio. Even in fairy tales, the princess needed to pull her weight, and in this case, there was no reason Sapphy couldn't contribute to this deal. Within minutes, she was pulling loose the knot she'd styled in her hair. SD shouldn't need the second location that was requested of them. It was a stall for time. There was something below the surface preventing Veronique Gautier from supporting the agreement, and she was going to learn what is was.

Sapphy pressed a button on the phone and requested that the receptionist connect her directly with Ms. Gautier. When the light on the base of her phone blinked, she retrieved the receiver.

"*Bonjour, Veronique. Cette Sapphy. Comment t'allez vous?*"

"Very well, Sapphy. Yourself?"

"Much better now that you're not holding me to continue speaking in French." Sapphy laughed into the phone. "I'm calling to invite you to coffee in the afternoon."

"Sounds wonderful, but I have a meeting that

won't be done before seven."

"How about a sunset drink at the Piazza by the bay? I'd really appreciate a little of your time this afternoon."

Determined to speak with the other woman face to face and discover the true problem in the negotiations that should been over long ago, she hoped Veronique would agree. They'd developed a good relationship, and Sapphy felt she could approach her and ask Veronique what was delaying the contract. It was the least she could do to contribute to SD.

"Perfect," Veronique agreed.

The women exchanged personal cell phone numbers and arranged a location to meet.

The moment their conversation ended, Sapphy's intercom buzzed.

"Signora Morelli, you have a call—"

"Thank you." She hit the button, and assuming Veronique had a question, she didn't request information about the caller.

"*Buongiorno*, Sapphyra."

Sapphy gagged on her sip of water, but forced herself to recover quick. "*Buongiorno*, Carmella. What can I do for you?" She said it out of manners, not a real desire to hear the conniving woman spin a new tale. Nothing was going to ruin Sapphy's mood, so she indulged Carmella.

"No, no, sweetheart. It is nothing like that." The septic sweetness in Carmella's tone turned Sapphy's stomach. "I am ringing you to apologize."

Releasing a slow, silent breath and holding back a laugh, Sapphy dropped her head into her hands and rubbed the bridge of her nose. "Apologize?"

"*Sì*. In the turmoil of yesterday's events, it may have looked as if I was upset or annoyed with you, my dear. Let me assure you, that was not the case or my intention."

What was it Dante had said? Typical Carmella? Sapphy couldn't care less about what the step-monster said. Not after this morning.

"We're fine. There is no reason to discuss this anymore."

"Yes, I realize that." Carmella paused, faking a cough. "I see that you were not being misled or taken advantage of. It was completely my mistake in thinking that Dante was doing anything else other than upholding appearances until the divorce is final. Thankfully, Dante and my daughter were upfront with you about the status of their relationship."

"No problem." It was a new setup. Sapphy wasn't falling for it. "There is no need to discuss this further."

"*Sì, bella.* I agree."

Divorziare! Finale!

Well, she wouldn't be so sure. "Don't count on it, dear step-monster," Sapphy breathed after she'd hung up. Yes. She was immune to Carmella and her interfering nature, but it didn't mean she couldn't resent the woman.

One more thing to take care of before Sapphy could relax with her new role. She picked up the phone and dialed Antonio's extension.

* * * *

Sapphy stood as Veronique rounded the building on the northern corner and approached. The women hugged and sat at the little round table on the piazza's edge.

"I'm glad you called and invited me," Veronique said, reaching across the metal tabletop. "It gave me the perfect reason to end the meeting on time."

"So happy I could be of some help." Sapphy

smiled, placing her hand over Veronique's. "But in the spirit of truth and new friendships, I need to be completely honest and admit I have a bit of a business agenda myself."

Veronique raised a shapely brow and tilted her head.

"However, that was not my only reason for inviting you. I'd really like to get to know you better, and I believe truly we'll enjoy each other's company," Sapphy added, making sure Veronique knew she was sincere. "We could table the business talk for now and start with the girl talk while we have the chance."

Veronique's shoulders relaxed. "That sounds nice. I'd like to put work aside for a few minutes and savor the lovely start to this evening." She picked up her glass and sipped wine the waiter had delivered. "Is your husband planning on joining us?"

"I don't think so," Sapphy said, dropping her gaze to her own glass. "He had a meeting in London this afternoon and isn't expected in Naples till late tonight."

The waiter returned, placed a variety of nuts between the ladies, and then told them to let him know when the two most beautiful women in the piazza needed more wine.

"Italian men are incredible flirts." Veronique laughed in a very sultry and French manner before waving him off.

"That is what I tell Dante," Sapphy added. "They are fantastic flirts, but they don't fake an attraction. You seem to have inspired a special twinkle in our waiter's eye."

"Ah, that would have been nice a few years ago," Veronique replied in a dreamy tone. "I'm afraid it is too late at this point in my life."

"Too late? No. It is never too late for love." Sapphy recognized the hurt embedded in Veronique's dark eyes, but couldn't agree. "You are young, beautiful, and very successful. Why would you give up on matters of the heart?"

"It was not my choice." Veronique sipped more wine and licked her lips, not bothering to disguise her distress. "I was married for almost ten years. I supported him while he established his career. I studied between juggling the two jobs I needed to in order to maintain a lifestyle he wanted to portray to acquaintances. Needless to say, I began my career well after he was successful."

"Dante mentioned you are divorced."

"Divorced?" Veronique pursed her lips as if sucking on a lemon. "More like disgraced." The elegant, beautiful, and powerful executive transformed into a vulnerable woman before Sapphy's eyes. "It's one thing to mutually end a relationship because it isn't working. It's another when you are the last one to know that your husband is sleeping with an unsavory woman and sharing professional secrets with her."

"I'm so sorry. That is very sad." Sapphy broke eye contact and glanced at her fingers. There was no real argument to that point. The situation was despicable.

"*Oui*," Veronique agreed in a raspy voice. "He shared the details of sensitive negotiations with an exotic dancer who had been hired by the competition. A stripper. A bimbette he couldn't converse with verbally, but was clearly able to communicate with."

"I'm sorry you had to go through that ordeal. It was your ex-husband's wrong doing, and it has no bearing on your character. You shouldn't lose hope. Not all men are like that." Strength and accomplishments didn't insulate a woman from such hurt, but it would be a shame to isolate oneself because of a dirt bag like her ex. Veronique shouldn't miss out on opportunities that could make her happy. She had too much to offer the world.

"*Non, non,* do not misunderstand. It is not his cheating or the divorce that has destroyed my belief in true love. It is the realities that we face as women in this world."

Not knowing how to answer, or whether she should answer, Sapphy nodded and raised her glass to her lips.

"You are in a very different position," Veronique continued. "Your husband is a force in the international community that is admired and feared. Dante is very focused on growing an empire that belongs to both of you, so it is in his best interest to support and guide you."

"He always has," Sapphy agreed.

"It is a benefit to have a man like Dante on your side when you enter a boardroom. It validates your presence." Veronique leaned across the table and motioned Sapphy to come close. "No matter how far women think they've come in the corporate world, it is still a man's domain. Men might tolerate us, but they don't like the fact that we are there. Some men put a target on our chest simply because we have one."

Sapphy shook her head. "I disagree, Veronique." She straightened and folded her arms on the table. "If anything, I believe men are intimidated by your keen business sense, not your sex. You are a woman, and you are very well respected in the board room."

"Not without a sacrifice. I can never trust a man to see me as a woman and not as a means to a self-serving end."

"That happened once. All men aren't the same."

Sapphy refused to believe that a woman as beautiful and smart as Veronique would only be a rung on a ladder for a man to use to hoist himself up. "Give it a chance, and your prince will come."

"You're a romantic. That is nice." Veronique raised her hand and motioned for the waiter. "I must admit that I was pleased to see you with Dante the other night. It isn't unusual for business acquaintances not to meet spouses, but I had heard about you and questioned why Dante had never spoken of you. I was wrong to doubt his integrity."

That was it. Veronique's personal bias had interfered with the deal. She thought that Dante was like her ex.

"So, you believed that a man who was dishonest to his wife would be dishonest in business with the ECL, and you delayed giving us the contract even though it is clearly in your benefit?" Sapphy asked.

"Perhaps. Subconsciously. Without being aware of doing it." Veronique confirmed Sapphy's suspicion.

"Who is the romantic, my friend?" Sapphy laughed and reached for her new friend's hand. "I can assure you, Dante is not dishonest. Our integrity is superior to any other companies. And, I have no complaints on how my husband treats me."

"After we met, it was apparent how he feels about you," Veronique said. "Sapphy, is this why you called? You wanted to know about the delay in the contract?"

"Yes. That was a big part of it." Sapphy looked into the other woman's eyes and did not dispute the truth. "It made no sense that the ECL didn't move faster to secure our company's services. I had to know why."

"Well, unofficially, you now know," Veronique said, like they had known and trusted each other for years. "But, I will never admit to it. It may not have been appropriate for the business world, but when dealing with a company that is run so tightly by its primary owner, his personal ethics affect the company's image and performance."

Using the same criteria, Veronique should have deduced that Dante's business practices were spotless. SD Holdings' reputation and growth had been stellar with him at the helm.

"Here is one more tip, and do not think that I disagree with your actions. I appreciate your honesty, but men think women are weak to investigate intuition. In this case, you were right, and by all means, your direct question on the delay settled my mind that I have made a good decision. A proposal is being delivered to Dante's office in the morning. I hope to have the deal signed by the afternoon."

Sitting back with relief, Sapphy thanked Veronique for her openness. She didn't blame her for her suspicions. If anything, she, too, applauded Veronique's intuition. She'd picked up on something nobody else had ever questioned.

"Would you prefer I send you the proposal?" Veronique asked.

"No. Dante has handled this from the start." Sapphy smiled and beckoned for the waiter. "Let's move on to girlfriend talk."

Ordering more wine and a margarita pizza to share, the women agreed to place business aside and enjoy the sunset.

"So," Veronique breathed in a casual tone. "How long have you and Dante been married?"

"Almost five years."

"You must have been a young bride."

"The circumstances that brought about our marriage were not the best." Sapphy blinked away the pain of her father's death, and told her companion about how both fathers had insisted that they marry.

"That explains why I didn't know of you earlier." Disappointment spread over the elegant French face. "Too bad. I thought I was able to read the love in your eyes for your husband the other night, and I had a small sliver of hope for the existence of a happy marriage—full of love."

"Just because we didn't marry in the traditional manner, and our ceremony was in a hospital chapel, doesn't mean there is no love. I've loved Dante forever."

Raising her glass, Sapphy wondered how honest she could be with the business shark that had morphed into a friend. "We're not speaking as business acquaintances?"

"Of course not, *mon ami*." Veronique shook her head and her coiffed bob swayed in a comforting manner. "We passed that line a few glasses ago."

"Good," Sapphy responded, settling in to a comfort zone for some truthful girl talk. "I've known Dante my whole life. It was the summer of my thirteenth birthday, when Dante gave me a fancy windsurfer that I realized how much I loved him."

"A windsurfer made you recognize your love?"

"Yes," Sapphy continued, swirling the wine in her glass and watching the tiny whirlpool. "He was so excited and tried to surprise me, but when I saw it, I burst into tears. You see, I was petrified of the water as a child."

A small sigh escaped Veronique, but she didn't speak.

"Dante made it his sole purpose for two weeks to make me feel comfortable on the board. He didn't go out with his friends, no parties, no clubs, and no soccer."

"That must have been difficult for a young man. He is older, no?" Veronique asked.

"Yes. He was seventeen. He spent all his time with me in one type of water or the other. Insisting that we swim in the deep end of the pool, he taught me all the strokes above the doggy-paddle." She smiled, recalling her resistance to getting wet and his insistence that landed them both in the water fully clothed. "Then in the afternoons, he'd take me to the beach on the fabricated premise that I was keeping him company. Morning, noon, and night he had me in the water. I thought my skin would never recover and that it would be permanently wrinkled."

"So," Veronique placed her chin on her propped hands and asked, "Did you get out on that windsurfer?"

"Heavens, no. That would mean I'd be out on the open water." Sapphy raised her hand and indicated for the waiter to bring more wine. "After I was comfortable with swimming, Dante insisted that I go sailing with him. Days with his determined arms wrapped around me, controlling a tiny sailboat, and countless picnics on a little quiet beach made me a very competent sailor. I learned to enjoy the sway of the sea and to crave the wind in my hair."

"That is wonderful." Veronique smiled and clapped her hands together. "I have never questioned Dante's determination. He managed to make you comfortable in what you feared."

The butterflies were back and filled her core with a sense of pride and accomplishment. "He made me love the water, not just feel comfortable with it."

"What a wonderful story of commitment. I can understand why you developed such grateful and thankful feelings toward Dante."

"Oh, there is much more." Sapphy placed her hand over her friends and stilled Veronique's drumming fingers. "It was the last day of summer," she continued, smiling to herself as she recalled the specifics. "Marco, Dante's father, threw Dante a big party to celebrate his leaving for university. There was a full moon in the sky, the breeze off the sea was warm, and the party was in full swing."

"He kissed you?" Veronique asked, sounding like a teenager.

"No. Nothing like that." Sapphy laughed and blushed. "He was too proper for that. You see, he still considered me a little girl."

"Oh, I doubt that," Veronique objected. "You were too young to see how he truly felt about you. Why do you think he spent all that time with you?"

"Anyway," Sapphy said, swatting the air. "At last, I thanked Dante for my birthday gift and told him that I couldn't wait to try it. I was ready. Without saying a word, he grabbed my hand and led me away from the festivities. He put me on the back of his motorcycle, shoved a helmet on my head, and drove straight to the beach. The windsurfer was waiting there. Ready to go out."

"*Mon Dieu.* Did he make you go in the water all dressed?"

"No, not Dante. He had it all planned." A low moan of pleasure escaped Sapphy's lips as she recalled the moment. "He had our suits in the BMW's storage compartment. Holding a towel around me, and always the gentleman, he looked the other way while I changed. Then he put on his suit, and we spent the entire evening on the windsurfer together. At first, he stood behind me. Later, when I was able to control the sail, he jumped off and swam near me. It was that very night that I knew I would love him forever."

"For a young man, he was unusually patient and good to you," Veronique agreed.

"I adored him, idolized him, but I was barely a teenager, and I knew that the time wasn't right for us." Sapphy scraped her teeth on her lower lip and continued to smile privately. "I was a child, and he was a man. I tried to grow up fast for him, but he wouldn't allow it."

Falling silent, Sapphy lost herself in the memories. Dante had always looked out for her, but it wasn't until now that their relationship was physical. Still, it was physical and romantic for reasons other than what Veronique implied. It was a business deal to secure the progress of SD, a business deal that had an expiration date that could leave Sapphy emotionally barren.

"Ah, but now, you are both mature, in love, and working together." Veronique sat back, entwining her long arms and stretching them ahead of her. "He would have asked you to marry him on his own if it hadn't happened the way it did."

The morning after the night on the windsurfer, Dante had brushed his lips over her forehead and whispered in her ear. *Don't worry, bambolina, I'll come back for you.*

* * * *

Dante spotted his wife and immediately instructed the driver to pullover. Yanking on the silver handle, he kicked open the door and hit the pavement before the driver had time to exit the car and come around as was customary.

Weaving his way through a group of tourists, Dante kept his eyes focused on the women sitting at the quaint table outside Aldo's. What was Sapphy doing with the woman who had the power to kill his

ECL agreement?

"*Ciao*, ladies," he called, adjusting his gate once Veronique spotted him and cocked her head his way.

Sapphy turned and smiled. Her welcoming expression and the depth of her gaze drew him in, and consumed all his attention. Placing his hand in the crook of her neck, he bent and claimed her lips as a reward. Her sweet and fresh female scent mingled with the sea air, filling his senses and stirring his libido.

"You're early," Sapphy breathed.

"A pack of wild dogs couldn't keep me away," he responded, brushing his lips over the side of her neck. "Why would I stay in London when I could be here with two beautiful women to watch the sunset?"

"Nicely put," Veronique said, placing her hand in his outstretched palm.

Dante bowed his head and raised her hand in a polite greeting. "What a pleasure to see you again, Miss Gautier."

"*S'il vous plaît*, I think that Sapphy and I are beyond such formal titles outside of working hours. And being that you are a significant part of my new friend, I'd appreciate it if you address me as Veronique and if I could refer to you as Dante."

"Done." Dante sat beside his wife and draped his arm across her shoulders, pulling her against him. "It is my pleasure."

The waiter approached and added a place setting for Dante. The threesome raised a glass to a wonderful sunset and settled into casual conversation.

"How did you know where to find us?" Sapphy asked.

"There was a note on the calendar on your desk. I called the penthouse, and when you weren't there, I figured you were still here. I wanted to surprise you."

"I'm glad you did," Sapphy said, placing her hand in his. Stroking her thumb over his knuckles, she smiled up at him and he had the urge to kiss her. He did—even if Veronique was there.

Sweeping his tongue gently over her warmth, he tasted wine on her lips. He'd missed her.

"Sapphy was telling me about the summer of her windsurfer," Veronique informed him. "So magical."

"The windsurfer?" He shifted in his seat and glanced at Sapphy. "You hated it."

"Maybe at first, but I grew to love it." Sapphy chuckled and looked out over the bay. "The sun is almost down. Look how beautiful the sky looks."

Dante didn't know what had happened to bring the women together, or why they had been discussing their childhood, but he knew he had to get Sapphy alone and learn exactly what transpired between the women. Did it have anything to do with the agreement?

"The two of you like this make me nervous," he joked. "I feel like I'm excluded from a special club or something."

The women laughed, and Dante found that he enjoyed Veronique's company outside the boardroom. Amused, he shook his head. He'd never expected that to be the case.

"Have you made plans for the weekend?" Dante asked.

Sapphy straightened and leaned toward Veronique. "Actually, in light of our new friendship, and the amazing comfort I feel with you, I have a favor to ask. I'd like to postpone the invitation for you to visit with us in Positano, if you don't mind. Family issues have surfaced and need immediate attention."

Alarm rang through Dante. It was rude to rescind

a personal invitation. "Sapphyra?"

"*Non, non, mon ami,*" Veronique covered Sapphy's hand in reassurance. "I would like to return to France myself, if things go as I foresee, but I would love to come back at a different time. A time for pleasure, not for business."

"I knew you'd understand. Thank you," Sapphy said and turned to Dante. "If we could arrange it, I would really like to go to New York this weekend."

Perplexed at the ease between the women, Dante nodded. It was as if they'd known each other for years and could communicate with eye signals to one another.

"Fantastic," Sapphy said, raising her shoulders and settling against him, more relaxed than he'd seen her in a long time. "Veronique, I have some great news to share with you."

The rest of dinner was spent discussing the developments with Andreas and the importance of family. Veronique was more than happy to reschedule her visit in lieu of the reunion, and the friends made plans for her to take a much needed break from work and join them in not only Positano, but on Zantè as well.

* * * *

Dismissing the driver for the night, Dante helped Sapphy out of the car and gathered her in his arms. Running his hand over her dark mane, he trapped the silky locks between his fingers as he lowered his mouth to hers.

"I missed you, *amore,*" he said, claiming her lips savoring her sweetness. "And now, I can't wait to get you alone and show you just how much." Grasping her hips, he pulled her against him and smiled when she gasped as his groin connected with hers.

"You'll have to wait until we get upstairs," she teased, nibbling on his jaw. "If not, we'll be giving the neighbors a show to remember."

Taking her hand, he rushed them indoors and directly to their private elevator. When the doors slid closed, he pushed her up against the mirrored wall and buried his face into the crook of her neck

"No one can see us here," he breathed. "I've been dreaming of making love to you all day. I've missed you, *cara mia.*"

He raised his mouth to hers and kissed her. She tangled her fingers in his hair and pulled him close. The ding of the elevator and the moan of pleasure escaping her lips were the two nicest sounds he had heard all day. He lifted her up, wrapped her calves around his waist, and carried her to their bedroom. All the while feasting on her mouth and refusing to let her go.

"I can't get enough of you," he said, placing his precious gift on the center of the bed. "You are so enticing, my beautiful Sapphyra."

Taking his time and enjoying the manner in which her body reacted to his touch, he gently removed each piece of her clothing. Her chest rose and sank quicker with each minute that passed. Heat collected on her golden skin beneath his fingertips. And her dusky nipples peaked under his visual caress, testing his resolve to go slow and tender.

Nude and smiling like a Greek goddess, she stretched and reached for his hand as he tossed aside her panties. "It is your turn," she said, using long elegant fingers to remove his cufflink.

She rose to her knees, and moving in a seductive dance, she approached him and undid each of his buttons in what seemed like a cruel amount of time.

His heart hammered and his groin tightened, and both were about to burst when she finally lowered her head and swept her tongue over one of his nipples.

"I missed you, too," she breathed.

Patience spent, Dante crushed her against his body. He needed her, wanted her, and desired her above anything in the world.

"I want you now," he groaned, placing her beneath him and taking her with unrestrained passion.

He buried himself inside her, and with each movement, felt more of his heart slipping into her hands. She was his and he would spend his days and nights making her happy. It was not out of responsibility or obligation. He would make her happy out of love.

Her body trembled and she looked into his eyes as her climax claimed her. With a final thrust, he released his passion in the woman he loved and joined her in a place of euphoria that was only theirs.

"*Ti amo*," he breathed, placing kisses on the side of her neck as he buried his face in her hair. *More than you could imagine, cara. More than I believed possible.*

Spent and satiated, they held each other and whispered dreams and desires to each other in the dark. Being with her was home. He was complete, and he knew that he would relive the past five years over and over in order to have the privilege of holding her in his arms.

They remained like that for a long time, in silence, reveling in each other's hold.

It was Sapphy who stirred much later, stretching and making the sweetest sounds as she repositioned herself in the massive bed.

"I think we'll be hearing from ECL in the morning," Sapphy said, snuggling against him.

"What did you do with Veronique? Arm wrestle her over it?"

"Funny." She pinched the taught skin on his abdomen and he yelped. "That should teach you to tease me when I'm trying to be serious and discussing business."

"*Cara*, I have no intention of discussing business with my naked wife in our bed," he said, pulling her over and fitting her atop his body. "We can do that when we are clothed and in the office."

He had two months to turn this business agreement personal. Two months to win her heart. He wasn't going to waste a minute.

They made love, and when she slept this time, he didn't stay awake and wonder what would happen between them. He knew that in the end, she would stay.

Chapter Nine

In the office, Dante reviewed the proposal on his desk and arranged to sign with Veronique in the afternoon. With the ECL discussions behind him, he would utilize all the executives he paid handsomely, leave the daily operations in their hands, and take his wife on an overdue honeymoon.

Antonio had reviewed the proposal with him and was in the process of drafting up the transfer of the Zantè deed to Eleni Petos. Dante was comfortable with the reports on the family, but he would suggest that Sapphyra delay the transaction for a little while. A comprehensive background check was needed before she did anything that gave up her rights to the family land that meant so much to her.

Dante called Cosmo in New York and requested that Sapphy's friend and confidant work with Antonio on the matter.

"I'm surprised she didn't tell me," Cosmo said.

"Well, she's been...preoccupied...since she found out," Dante replied, grinning at the double meaning. His wife was busy. She had turned into a little workaholic that mixed business with pleasure with the greatest finesse. If it wasn't for her lingering jetlag, he doubted that he would have been able to sneak out of the penthouse without her in the morning. Knowing her body required more rest, he had to put her needs first.

* * * *

It was almost nine o'clock when Sapphy opened her eyes. Squinting against the morning sun streaming in through her window, she stretched her arms over her head and her fingers found a sheet of paper on Dante's pillow with his script on it.

> *Good morning, Bella.*
> *I'm sorry I didn't see you open your gorgeous eyes, but I have an early appointment in the office. I'll miss you. I've instructed the staff not to do any noisy cleaning. They should be done by nine, if not earlier.*
> *Call me when you wake.*
> *Dante*

No love.
No kisses and hugs.
Just Dante.

Maybe he had been in a rush to make his meeting. She shrugged, holding the note against her naked breast. They didn't fall asleep till four in the morning, and last night's events certainly hadn't suggested that he didn't care.

Whispering words of adoration, he'd held her, kissed her, and pleasured her body and soul, tirelessly through the night. It was she who had drifted off to sleep after the third time they'd made love.

Not caring if it wasn't proper and easy, she planned to discuss their future openly with him. A good marriage was based on proper communication, so she would ask the questions that mattered and not assume that he loved her.

Pulling the covers off, she dropped her legs over the side of the bed and rose to a sitting position. There, on her nightstand, sat a cup of café Americano and two chocolate biscotti on the saucer- the breakfast Sapphy preferred. He must have brought in the coffee before he left because it was too cold to drink. She made a mental note to thank him anyway. What a pleasant surprise to learn of Dante's domestic talents.

Sapphy showered, and then wrapped in a plush bathrobe, made her way into the kitchen. No staff was around.

She made a fresh cup of coffee to enjoy at Dante's desk while she reviewed the work she'd brought home with her for last night and never got to. More clients and files to acquaint herself with would make the office transitions much easier.

She dialed headquarters and asked to speak to Dante.

"I'm sorry, Sapphyra. Dante is in a meeting and has asked not to be disturbed. He did tell me to inform you that he'll be available at three. I will ask him to call as soon as he is done," Gabriella offered.

Sapphy told her not to bother. She'd be in by noon. Sapphy calculated the time in New York. Cosmo rarely went to sleep like a normal person. She sent him a text, and he called back before she'd made herself comfortable at the desk.

"I knew you'd be up. No way would you be in bed this early," she said. First, she asked about her friend's father, and then she told him all about her meeting with Veronique and their conversations.

"Wow, Sapphy. It seems Italy has really opened you up," Cosmo said. "You rarely trusted anyone in

New York. You think that you should be so honest with this woman?"

"Cosmo, she's a friend. A real friend. I can feel it in my bones." Sapphy plopped onto the office chair and spun around as if she had no cares in the world. "Besides, there is nothing wrong with my relationship with Dante. Nothing I need to hide."

"It's safe to say that things are going well with Dante?"

"No," she replied, joy flirting over her. "Things are going great. He's amazing, and it looks like he's happy that I'm his wife. All he needs is some time to get used to all of this true marriage stuff and having me around." She cooed into the phone like a high school girl. "I'm so in love with him, Cosmo."

Cosmo's deep laughter was a welcomed pause to her confession. She knew it sounded sappy, but the truth was just that: the truth. And this time, she was more than happy with it.

"I don't think it is time that Dante needs," Cosmo said. "He loves you, Sapphy. You have to be blind not to see that."

Clasping the cordless phone, Sapphy stood, paced the room, and kicked at the imaginary stars at her toes.

He'd said it again last night. Dante had said he loved her as he made love to her.

"Earth to Sapphy..." Cosmo's voice carried over the distance.

"I'm here," she breathed into the mouthpiece.

"Did you get the last part?"

She shook her head. "What was that?"

"He's been waiting on you," Cosmo repeated. "You have it all in your hands to decide where the two of you end up. Talk to the man and put him out of his misery. Be honest."

"I think you might have a point, counselor. I'm doing it tonight." She dropped onto the chair and swiveled it around again. "I need to finish reviewing some files before I go to the office."

"You're home?"

"Yeah, we had a late night and I didn't hear the alarm in the morning. Dante didn't wake me when he left." A sense of pleasure filled her chest at the remembrance of the events leading up to her sitting at home and sipping her coffee.

"Sounds like things are going better than you think, *koukla*. I'm happy for you."

"Thanks," she said, flying on air from the realization.

"I have an admission for you," Cosmo said, clearing his throat. "I spoke with Dante earlier today, and he told me about Petos. Were you going to get around to telling me that you've found your father's sister any time soon?"

"Sure," she whispered and laughed. "If you were only patient for ten seconds longer, I would have gotten around to that." She stood and paced the room.

"You need to be careful and verify that Petos is who he says he is," Cosmo cautioned.

"I know, I know," she said. "Antonio gave me the same speech yesterday."

There was a long, uncomfortable pause on the line. She could imagine Cosmo rolling his eyes and preparing a lecture.

"Listen, I may be over stepping my bounds, but this guy shows up out of the blue and is suddenly all over your personal and literal business," Cosmo said, sounding worried. "If you don't want to involve Dante, do you want me to hire that Personal Investigator we spoke about?"

"I'm not going to rush and sign the deed over until the normal investigations are complete." She was smarter than that, and this was too important to work solely off her gut feelings. "But, Cosmo, I know there is nothing wrong here. Petos is family. I'm simply waiting to meet Thea Eleni and carryout my father's wishes directly with her. We'll be in New York over the weekend. Make time for me."

"Will do, Sapphy. I'll see you in a few days."

The call ended, and she attempted to work through the remainder of the files.

She was almost done with the pile when the elevator hummed to life. Glancing past the office door and across the living area, her heart jumped with joy when Dante entered. He carried two large tan canvas bags in his broad embrace.

"I thought you were in a meeting?" Sapphy asked.

"I was." Dante placed the bags on the glass table and shrugged his jacket off his broad shoulders. "I can end the meetings when I chose. One of the perks of sleeping with the boss," he said, pulling off his tie and striding to where she stood with a big grin on his handsomely sculpted face.

With one hand, he unbuttoned his crisp white shirt and revealed the tanned, muscled skin beneath it, causing her to lick her lips in anticipation. With the other, he pulled her against him and whispered how he could only think of her naked body sprawled all alone in bed.

Sapphy's heart beat fast and her skin heated under his touch as his lips caressed the curve of her shoulder. This was the noon break she'd wanted her whole adult life. Dante had come home to her.

"Unless you mind," he added, in a gruff, hungry tone. "I'd like to enjoy my lunch with you." Slipping a possessive hand under her robe, he brought his palm to rest on her hip.

Her fingers splayed on the back of his neck as their lips met and the demanding request of his mouth ended in a kiss.

"I guess all employees can use some time away from the office," she said, flipping her hair and offering a sensual invitation in the form of a smile.

Laughter rumbled from deep within his chest as he lifted her in his arms and carried her to the bedroom while the bodily assault on her being continued. Lowering her feet to the floor, he pulled on her belt and allowed the robe to fall open.

"You are so beautiful," he said, guiding the soft material off her shoulders and watching it collect at her feet as it dropped. "Actually, you're perfect."

A large hand cupped her breast, and then his lips closed on hers and stole the thoughts from her mind. Her world consisted of the man in her arms, the man who drummed life into her body with each stroke of his fingers over her sizzling skin. Battling with her desire to offer herself immediately and completely at that very moment, she took a step back and admired his appearance. Casual, yet strong. Tender, yet sexy.

He was perfect!

"Ts, ts," she breathed, shaking her finger at him and pointing to his pants, then his shoes. "Here I am, nude and exposed, and you look like you're in the boardroom."

He kicked off his shoes, dropped his pants, and shucked off his underclothes in less than a minute. His erection, full and at attention, indicated that the boardroom was not on his mind.

"I'm glad you're here," she breathed, treasuring the feel of his bare skin as he drew her into his arms.

"We have some things to discuss before we return to the office."

He raised his dark head and gazed at her eyes. "Unless you believe it is necessary at this very moment, I just want to kiss you." His lips seared a path over her chest to her belly. "I want to make love to you." His hands feathered across her thighs and his hot breath followed their lead. "And, I absolutely do not want to discuss business until I have satisfied every other desire you may possibly have."

Sapphy's fingers tangled in his hair as Dante kissed each thought of everything and anything but him away. She moaned and arched her body against him, allowing the heat from his every touch to permeate the deepest areas of her heart.

"Maybe, I am selfish," Dante whispered. "But, I cannot help myself. All day long, I thought of being with you. I have not been able to concentrate on anything but the sweet taste of your lips, the sensual scent of your skin, and the exquisite feel of your hands. I must satiate this need for you before I could function on any other level."

Her legs wrapped around his hips and invited him to enter a world of ecstasy that only he shared with her. He suckled a taught nipple as if feasting on their passion, as his tongue encouraged the quivers of delicious desire to overtake her.

Slowly, he entered her warmth and groaned when her hips rose and her muscles clamped around him. She was gone. Flying in a place that was pure perfection.

He was her completion. She was his wife. He was her heaven. And Sapphyra was all his, body, soul, and heart.

Her nails scraped over his back, and her mouth

closed on his shoulder as the climax shot through her body. That was all the encouragement he needed, and with one final thrust, he released himself deep within her, filling her with warmth and love.

She loved him.

Snuggling against her husband, she closed her eyes and prayed a silent prayer of gratitude.

When their breathing calmed, Dante rolled to his side and propped himself on his elbow. Her gaze swept over him, igniting more flames of passion with what she saw. He shook his head and pushed her tousled hair away from her face, cupping her cheek and grinning like a young boy eyeing his dessert.

"I have the perfect boss," he said, brushing his lips over her mouth.

Sapphy agreed, kissing him back. Her tongue searched his delicious mouth, while her fingers trailed down his arm, over his chest, and against his abdomen. He stilled her hand.

"If you continue with that type of exploration, I'll never get back to work, and I won't be able to provide for our food and shelter," he teased.

"Food." She bolted up. "That's right." She dragged the sheet from under them. "I forgot to eat this morning, and you're hungry."

"I have all the sustenance I need right here. With you." He captured her wrist and brought her hand to his mouth, placing a heated kiss on the center of her palm. "It is you who needs to eat and keep your strength up." His thumb outlined the edge of the sheet draped over her breasts. "You will need it for later. I cannot seem to get enough of you, *bella*."

"I'm not complaining," she said, playing along and purring under his touch. "You're sort of appetizing yourself."

Grinning like a madman, he let her hand go and scooted her off the bed. "Come on, you wicked and enchanting woman. I stopped at the trattoria on the way home."

They ate, showered, made love, and showered again.

Since she had no appointments and no meetings scheduled, she decided to work from the penthouse the remainder of the day. They agreed that she'd meet him at headquarters at five, and he would brief her on the day's events.

"I promise to have good news when I see you," he said as he set up a link to the office computer with her laptop.

"About?"

"No." He smacked his lips and shook his head. "I will see you in the office."

She shrugged and casually sauntered away. He took her hand and twirled her around to face him "I can't wait. It seems now that things have changed, my patience and self-control have evaporated. I need to tell you now."

Encouraging him to continue, she smiled and held his hand.

"We are investing in a tiny village twenty-five kilometers out of the city-center. The village has been practically abandoned and there are only a few residents left there. With the infusion of work opportunities being made available, the mayor believes the young people will return and refurbish the family homes."

"That is perfect. You always find something better than the original plan," she replied, giving him a hug as he straightened from the desk.

"The concept is very popular all over Europe.

Corporations are locating in the countryside and reestablishing villages that would be ghost towns without them."

"I'm aware of the trend." Sapphy's face was bright with happiness. "I really like the idea. I'm thrilled with it."

"I thought you would be. That is why I couldn't wait to tell you about it. I left a file in the office with the details for you." Standing, he brushed his lips over her mouth, but didn't linger. "I need to go."

Sapphy nodded. "We also need to discuss my aunt and Andreas. I want to transfer the Zakynthos property to her."

He kissed her forehead, and then picked up his briefcase. "I really must go. I have a meeting in twenty minutes."

"If you must..." She allowed her voice to trail seductively as she ran a finger down his tie.

"I better go while I can still walk." He laughed and shook his head as he strolled into the elevator. "Maybe you should wait for me here. In bed."

"I'll think about it." She smiled as she blew him a kiss and the doors slid shut. He did love her. She knew it. There was no question in her mind.

Wrapping her arms across her stomach, she squeezed to seal in her joy and ignored the tear rolling down her cheek. It was a tear of elation and there was no reason to wipe it away.

Her cell phone sang out *New York, New York*. She raced to the office to speak to Cosmo.

"So far, so good. A Dionysius and Maria Petos arrived on Ellis Island with a young toddler named Eleni in the mid forties. Some of the records, and they're slim, suggest that the parents may have been blood relatives. Maybe that is why they didn't have biological children. We can't be sure, but it seems to fit, Sapphy. They were born in Zakynthos and escaped during the occupation."

"I know it's her." Sapphy scraped her teeth over her lower lip, unable to come to terms with her good fortune. "You and Antonio could have your goons do all the research you want. I have the proof in Andreas's eyes. They are a replica of my father's eyes."

"You didn't mentioned that before," Cosmo cautioned. "It wasn't so obvious when you met with him in the Union."

"We were sitting by the window, and he kept his sunglasses on." She strolled to the office and glanced at the messy desk. "How does a man, who keeps his life in perfect order, have a desk that looks like an earthquake hit?"

"What?"

"Nothing," she dismissed the thought, shaking her head. "Hey, do what you have to do. I'm not wrong about Andreas, but I'm also not in any rush. I understand the arguments about verifying all the facts, but I'm just letting you know that I, personally, don't need more to know."

"As long as you're willing to be reasonable and wait a few days," Cosmo said, topping it off with an exaggerated sigh. "You're right. We'll take care of the legwork. You—meet the lady. Get to know the family. By then, we'll have all the information we need."

"Fine. Now let me go and get to work. You need to get some sleep, and I have to do some research on an industrial village SD Holdings will be establishing for the ECL."

"So you like the idea?" Cosmo asked, obviously in the loop.

"No," she replied. "I love it."

Cosmo laughed and finished the conversation with a promise to meet in Little Italy for lobster tails and cappuccinos on the weekend.

Just when I thought things couldn't get any better...lobster tails! Yum. Sapphy gingerly dropped onto a pile of files in the chair, leaned back, placed her feet on the edge of the desk, and crossed them at the ankles.

"Mrs. Dante Morelli," she said aloud. "I like that even more."

It had been an incredible morning, an amazing lunch, and now, she had a few hours to learn about the future of an investment she ached to work on. Time to get down to business.

She searched the pile to the left and found nothing on the industrial village. The pile on the right yielded the same empty results. Then, she stubbed her toe on a stack on the floor beside her chair and bent to retrieve it.

For the powerhouse Dante is, he is an absolute slob at home. How does he ever find things in this mess?

Placing the folders on the desk, she leaned her head to the side in order to read the labels. One with her name on a bright blue tab drew her immediate attention.

"Found it."

Making room on the leather blotter, she pulled the folder from the pile and opened it.

Her heart stopped.

Tears blurred her vision.

The room spun like a top. Red. Gold. Brown. Furniture, walls, floor, and light blended into one endless smear of pain.

She moaned as the printed pages slipped to her feet. Covering her face, she ground out a wounded sound against her hands and released the last bit of air in her lungs.

Stupid!

She'd been so stupid. What was that old American saying? Don't assume. You make an *ass* out of *u* and *me*. And that was exactly what she was: an ass!

She'd changed the plan and hadn't made her intentions clear to all parties involved. She hadn't told Dante what she wanted. She'd failed on reading the complete situation and she missed the big picture. Yes, she'd failed. Her degrees may as well stay buried in the drawer. How many classes had she taken on management, and how many times had the professors stressed that proper communication was the most important element in an efficient company?

Theé mou. She was being ridiculous. Did any of this really matter when the elephant of despair sitting on her chest had her struggling to breath? She dropped her head between her legs to prevent the world from going dark. She wouldn't faint. Tears flowed like a river after a storm and sobs rocked her body.

She'd done this. She'd put herself in the position to get hurt. If only she'd kept her distance, Dante would have completed his duty with no physical involvement. She was the immature partner who didn't know how to handle her professional and personal life. But it was done, and she'd need to learn to cope with all the consequences. There was too much at stake with their common company interests to fail—again.

Once she was able to inhale without fighting to force the oxygen into her chest, she opened her eyes and stared at the sticky yellow arrows on the papers at her feet. They marked where she should sign: on the dotted line beneath Dante's signature.

She snatched the sheets off the floor, put them in

order and searched the desk for a pen. Clutching the smooth thick, black barrel between her fingers, she stared through the moist blur and bit her lip till the taste of blood registered in her numb mind. Not bothering to read the fine print, she signed in each spot and placed the sheets in the folder.

Running her fingers through her hair, she massaged her scalp and instinctively glanced at the file that had shattered her perfect world. Tears followed her gaze and sealed away the happiness she'd experienced the past few days, as well as the happiness she'd been expecting for the future. Sapphy dropped her head and placed her palms on the desk as she rocked on the pile she sat upon. Allowing a few extra seconds for her trembling to stop, she fought the tears and formulated her plan of action.

Sapphy reached for the phone and made arrangements.

She'd go to New York and take care of the family situation on her own. It would allow her the time needed to compose herself, to put on her big-girl panties, and to accept that the domestic relationship with Dante was simple sex. After all, she was the one who had insisted on exclusivity and had offered herself to the man. Going into it, she knew there was no guarantee that she could win his love and alter their course for the divorce.

So, it was on to plan B: Work beside the man, and maximize their business potential. If she put distance between them for a few days, she'd be stronger to deal with it when she returned.

Chapter Ten

The torrent of rain released from the heavens on the pretty city by the bay, reflected Sapphy's mood as she transferred from the gate to the awaiting jet. Being that she had never before requested the use of the company jet, she wasn't sure of the procedure, but Antonio had met her at the airport and escorted her to the tarmac.

"Are you positive you don't want to wait for the reports to be finalized, Mrs. Morelli?" Antonio asked.

"Oh, Antonio, cut the Mrs. Morelli stuff. You were the one who snuck me my first, and last, cigarette when I wanted to try smoking." She sighed, running her finger over the pattern the rain made on the windowpane.

"I rolled a really thick and sloppy cigarette," he said, chuckling. "You never asked for one again."

She rolled her eyes, gaining comfort from his playful tone. "Just call me Sapphy, like you always have."

"*Sì*, Sapphy."

Antonio had been Dante's best friend since forever. He, too, never backed away from a chance to be a big brother.

He placed his hand on hers and gave it a long squeeze. "I will talk to my friend, and not my client, at this moment." His solemn gaze met hers and held. "You shouldn't make any decisions when you are upset."

"Who said I'm upset?"

He grinned and made a peculiar sucking noise between his teeth with his tongue—showing her what he thought of her ridiculous question. Antonio always did that to break the tension and make her smile. Usually, he succeeded at getting her to laugh and give him a small tap on the arm, but not today. She simply turned back to look at the grey sky.

"You are upset, so do not try to hide it. It is as evident as the red rings under those pretty blue eyes of yours."

She shook her head, negating his observation.

Kissing her cheek, he released her hand. "Then go safely and come back quickly. The plane is waiting for you."

The driver opened her door, and she withdrew from the comfort of her friend's company. The downpour had dropped the temperature, and the afternoon was more like fall than early summer. She shrugged and followed the driver up the metal staircase without looking back. She needed to get away.

"Mrs. Morelli," the captain greeted her at the jet's entrance. "It is a pleasure to be flying you to New York today."

She nodded politely and looked past him into the cockpit. All the dials were lit up and the co-pilot was communicating with someone on a headset.

"Rosalia is your attendant," the pilot added. "She will take you to Mr. Morelli. He is in the main cabin. I will report to you before we depart."

Mr. Morelli? Sapphy bit her lip. How could that be?

Rosalia appeared from behind a curtain and introduced herself. Guiding Sapphy through the cabin, she gave her a tour of the jet's amenities. There was a complete conference room bolted to the floor, equipped with a full-sized table and eight swivel chairs. Next, they passed a door, much like the one for the cockpit, marked Private. Rosalia said that was Mr. Morelli's private suite, but Sapphy refused the suggestion to look in.

Dante sat, cross-legged in the salon area with a drink in his hand. He stood as Sapphy approached and fixed her with a stern look. Taking two steps forward, he cupped her face and sank his fingers into her hair. His lips captured hers, and he took his time with the intimate greeting, oblivious to the fact that Rosalia was standing beside them.

Emotional confusion plagued Sapphy's heart and mind as she pushed against his chest to end the kiss.

"Thank you, Rosalia," Dante said to the attendant. "I will let you know if we need anything before takeoff."

Rosalia nodded and walked toward what Sapphy assumed was the galley area in the back of the plane. It was clear that Dante was not in the mood for small talk and no employee would dare infringe on his space. Both pilots and the attendant made themselves scarce.

"We, as you so clearly point out, are married and husband and wife in every sense of the word." Dante's dark gaze bore into her, alerting the tiny hairs on her arms to stand at attention. "When there is something so important we must do in our lives, we do it together. *Capisci?*"

She was trying to keep her heart safe from him. How was she supposed to do that when they were together?

Pelting the streamlined jet without a break, the rain mimicked the staccato rhythm of her heartbeat. The thunder hit in tandem with her distress. She didn't speak.

A handset on the seat where Dante had been sitting rang, and he answered it. Replying in Italian, he informed the pilot that they were not in a hurry, and of course, they would need to wait for the weather to stabilize before taking off. Offering Sapphy the seat next to his, Dante concluded his conversation and requested a snack be brought to them in half an hour.

Sapphy met his pensive gaze. "But, your meeting with Veronique—"

"Taken care of." He waved his hand and settled it on her thigh. "Now tell me, why would you leave without me for New York? I thought we agreed to go the end of the week."

The compassion and understanding that replaced the sternness in his voice was twice as unsettling for Sapphy. It made it much more difficult to keep the barrier erected and that made her more vulnerable.

Raising her shoulders, she sighed and sank into the comfort of her seat. If she was going to make this partnership successful, she couldn't let her heart get in the way. A physical relationship didn't constitute devotion and love, but an admission of her disillusionment would scar their professional relationship.

Big girl panties. Put them on and deal with it.

"It was an impulse decision to go today. I didn't want to distract you from the ECL deal," she lied, dropping her gaze so the mockery of the situation wouldn't be apparent. "There is no need for both of us to go to New York to meet my family."

"Of course there is," he replied, lifting her chin with his thumb and gazing into her eyes. "Your family is my family, *bambolina*. We are one, and anything that is important to you is important to me. I will always be by your side when you confront situations vital to your happiness and future."

Dante never abandoned his duties and obligations, but soon, he wouldn't need to concern himself with her. She would assume all her personal responsibilities on her birthday. Legally and morally, he would be released of any duties from their marriage contract. The divorce papers would be finalized with the courts in a few weeks, and he would be truly free of her, less the business arrangements. She didn't want to think or dwell on her predicament any longer.

In the mean time, she needed to maintain the peace and let things ride. It wouldn't serve either of them to argue over details that had been settled five years earlier. And sex, well, sex was just that. A physical act of a married couple that she had invited with no urging on his part. She had to accept it for what it was for Dante: a physical release, not an emotional testament of his love.

Sapphy swallowed past the knot in her throat. Life wasn't a fairy tale after all, but she had to play her part. Being the princess for three months would have to be enough

"Dante, thank you for joining me," she whispered, folding her legs beneath her and snuggling against her seat's shelter. "I'm tired and would like to rest for the flight."

Lame excuse, but she didn't care. She needed insulation from her feelings until she adjusted to the reality of her relationship with Dante.

"Okay, *bambolina*." He tucked his jacket around her shoulders. "We'll move to the suite after we are in the air. It shouldn't be long."

She repressed the urge to cringe as he brushed his lips over hers and smiled empathetically. Damn, why was it so difficult to separate his kindness toward her from her love for him? Why did she want so much more than he gave freely? And how was she going to survive what was left of her marriage?

Battling to calm her nerves, Sapphy shut her eyes. She was overreacting and making this a very difficult situation. If she were mature, she would accept it as part of the contract and plan her life accordingly. Scraping her teeth over her lip, she pulled his jacket under her chin and inhaled his scent. The crisp, clean, masculine essence of the man she loved was embedded in the material, and ironically, gave her more comfort than she cared to admit.

The rhythmic drumming of the rain and the ache deep within her chest synchronized and lulled her into a dark place, offering her peace from the turmoil of the day's discovery. She drifted off to sleep.

Dante studied her angelic face, as the stress lines faded and her breathing finally grew soft. He hadn't seen her so distraught and upset in a long, long time, and he didn't know how to help. How could he if he saw no logical reason for her reaction?

Antonio hadn't exaggerated when he'd expressed his concern over Sapphy's rapid change of plans and had informed Dante of her trip. It was a good thing she'd requested the paperwork for her aunt's inheritance, because that was the only way Dante had learned of her impromptu travel. She certainly hadn't shared her plans, and the pilot hadn't alerted Dante about the flight. He planned on addressing that important omission before they landed. Perhaps she shared the same corporate title, but more than being his partner, she was his wife.

Running his hands through his hair, Dante massaged his throbbing head and tried to see the situation from Sapphy's point of view. He racked his brain for the cause of her distress, but he kept coming up empty. There seemed to be no explanation, or at least none that he was aware of, for the abrupt change in her disposition. She'd shut down her emotions and didn't let him near. It was as if she didn't want to be close to him, or as if she'd changed her mind about their future together.

Pinching the bridge of his nose, Dante rested his elbows on his knees. He really hadn't sensed anything was wrong. For him, everything seemed to be going according to plan. Their lifelong connection blossomed into what he thought was a comfortable and honest relationship. Sapphy's return gave him more pleasure than he would have ever thought, and their business posed no problems. She was with him after all these years, and he was able to hold her in his arms like he'd wanted to since the first day they were married. He didn't understand what had happened to put that frown on her face.

Unless—unless, she didn't want him. He rubbed his temples harder as he recalled the afternoon she'd stormed into his meeting. She'd strutted into the conference room in battle mode, and then she'd informed him in private that they needed to execute their business agreement and their divorce. She'd wanted to move on with her life. Not their life. Sapphy had planned on the divorce.

Accidenti! I've been dense. Acting like a teenager, letting raging hormones make decisions, and all the time, I have not listened to what she said.

She wanted out, and their physical coming together complicated things for her. That was why she withdrew from him. Not wanting to deal with the complication, she opted to run.

His throat constricted. He couldn't believe that after all he'd offered her she was turning away from him. He wasn't going to allow it. He'd proven his worth to her. He'd taken their company to new heights, and he'd established himself as a capable and dependable husband. He wasn't a carefree womanizer like the newspapers had portrayed him when they were first married. Fisting his hands, he restrained himself from shaking her to see reason—to accept him.

No. He wouldn't make it easy for her this time. Sapphy was his wife, and she'd agreed to act as such. There were two months left to make her change her mind, and he'd let her know, in no uncertain terms, what he expected and wanted from her. He wouldn't let her walk away.

Dante settled in his seat, resisting the need to gather her in his arms and carry her to the suite so that they could discuss things, or argue over them, if necessary. After all, married couples argued all the time. However, he didn't want to risk waking her and waste the few hours he had to organize his plan. When Dante wanted something, he secured every detail to guarantee the outcome.

Working on his laptop, Dante pounded out explicit instructions for the flight crew, delegated assignments to company executives, and cleared his calendar until the end of the month. No unnecessary interruptions. He would keep Sapphy in his sight for every waking and sleeping moment.

He emailed Cosmo, knowing it was still very early in New York, and requested he meet them at the airport upon arrival. They would need to review the details on the property transfer Sapphy was bent on completing quicker than Dante was comfortable with. She was proving to be much more impatient than she portrayed herself to be.

To his surprise, Cosmo replied immediately.

I've compiled a full report and will present it to you when we meet. In my opinion, Mrs. Petos is the real deal.

-Young family of three: father, Dionysius Potamis, mother, Vassiliki Potami, and their young daughter, Eleni, arrived on Ellis Island in 1945.

-Written records in Zakynthos are non-existent.

-There are confirmations from eyewitnesses about formal adoption that fits with Andreas's story.

-Eleni Petos wants nothing but to meet her niece and to visit the family home.

-One concern: Andreas wishes to host her seventieth birthday party on the island. It appears like genuine family interest, but this may be an issue if disputes arise. What do you think?

-IMO: There appears to be no selfish motivation for the contact. At present, they haven't placed claim on the patriarchal property.

Will meet you at the airport early tonight, and you can review the documentation and decide for yourselves.

Have a good flight.
Cosmo

Cosmo, also, appeared sincere and genuine when it came to his concern for Sapphy and her welfare. Perhaps Dante owed him a thank you for being a true friend.

Glancing at his wife, he couldn't suppress the smile forming on his lips. Maybe it wasn't her original intention, but she was going to love being Mrs. Morelli. Dante retrieved Cosmo Papodopoulos's personal file. He'd make a point of getting to know his wife's friend. Not only did he owe it to Cosmo, but it would make Sapphy happy and more accepting.

Once the jet was at cruising levels, the pilot entered the cabin and apologized for the mishap and 'non'-communication on the trip.

"I was unaware of your desire to have personal reports on every flight the corporate jet was scheduled for, but I do understand your request where Mrs. Morelli is concerned. I promise my full personal attention to any flights regarding your wife," the captain assured Dante. "I can only say that I viewed it on a corporate level and was following Mrs. Morelli's instructions for discretion."

"I can see why you didn't contact me," Dante said. "But anything concerning my wife should immediately be brought to my attention. After all, captain, you'd want to same where your wife is concerned."

"Such a mistake won't happen again." The captain nodded in understanding and grinned when Dante accepted his apology. "It is safe to transfer signora to your private quarters for a good night's rest."

Dante thanked the man, who his father had hired as the first pilot in their corporate fleet, and then dismissed him, a bit more empathetic about the pilot's position due to Sapphy's request for privacy with the flight.

Dante turned his attention back to his laptop as the crew performed their duties for the trans-Atlantic flight. Typically, they flew to the States through the daylight and arrived in the afternoon. This trip had originated in the early evening, so they'd be arriving at night, which should make it a little easier to acclimate themselves to the time difference if they managed to stay awake for the flight.

Once again, Dante's gaze settled on his sleeping wife. Perhaps her forehead wasn't littered with stress lines, but turmoil was dancing within her. With her knees drawn up to her chest, her arms folded about her legs, and her shoulders huddled over, she had totally cocooned herself. The message was clear: *Stay away, and don't touch me.*

His chest tightened as his mind played with the thought of being apart from her. He'd allowed their separation for too long, and he wasn't willing to put himself in a similar situation again. Forcing the air into his lungs, he decided that Sapphy was not sleeping through the flight. They needed to talk—needed to figure out the rest of their lives. Dante wasn't making any assumptions and chancing losing her.

She was part of him. She had been for a very long time. He was part of her. He'd waited patiently for her to realize that they belonged together and to come to him on her own accord. And, she had. He wasn't going to let her change her mind. Not now, not ever.

"Wake up, *bambolina*." He skimmed his knuckles down her satin cheek, and his heart dropped as she recognized it was Dante and flinched. He swallowed the hurt of the rejection and cleared his throat. "Sapphy, please wake up so we can talk," he said in a calmest voice he could conjure.

"I'm tired," she mumbled. "I want to sleep."

"No." He shook his head. "I'm sorry. You must wake up."

She opened her eyes and glanced at him. She quickly recoiled and her lashes dropped, shielding the mirrors of her soul from his view. The asphyxiating veil of tension between them was impossible for him to accept. The barrier needed to come down.

"Sapphy, I want to discuss a few things with you. Please look at me," he insisted.

She moaned, but refused to open her eyes. The defensive bubble around her grew as she turned to face the window and gathered her shoulders tight into her body. His patience and understanding slipped, and he wanted nothing but her full attention.

"Sapphyra, wake up. Now."

Once again, lines creased her forehead and her eyelids lifted. As if with great effort, she looked at him with anxious blue eyes, wrenching his heart in the way a towel was rung out in the wash. He pushed the heel of his palm against his chest and took a deep breath.

"What is it, Dante?" Sitting straight in the chair, she assumed a business persona, but it was impossible to hide the apprehension in her body. Her chest rose and fell too sharply, her slender fingers played at the hem of her sweater, and her denim-clad legs bounced a bit too fast.

"It will be much easier to adjust to the jetlag if we can stay awake throughout the flight." He offered an opportunity for them to stay awake and chat. "Would you like to move into our quarters and enjoy dinner in private?"

Knowing Sapphy since the moment she was born, he knew that forceful words would only make her combative. He wasn't looking for a fight. He had to win over her heart. And, he had to do it fast. There were a little over two months that she would have to honor their agreement. He would succeed.

"No."

"Excuse me?" Shock pierced his demeanor. She'd never been abrupt or rude.

"I'm good." Unfolding and refolding her legs, she rearranged herself in her neat cocoon.

Furious, he wanted to pull her into his arms, carry her to his bed and show her exactly how much she was to him. But when she turned her back to him again, desire and shock collided, forming a red cloud within him denser than annoyance.

"Cut the drama, Sapphyra. We are going into our quarters to talk."

Chapter Eleven

There was no way Sapphy could avoid him. She'd pretended to sleep, but he'd insisted she wakeup. She'd turned her back to him, but he'd asked her to look at him. Then, she flat out said 'no', and still, he demanded the talk.

What the hell was she going to tell him? *Sorry, Dante. I made a mistake. I'm not strong enough to let you play with my body while you trample my heart. I thought that you loved me, too. Do you want the divorce papers now or later?*

Motioning for Rosalia, Dante stretched his legs and stood. "Please have the chef prepare the cappelini and the pork filet. When it is ready, ring my suite."

Rosalia bowed her head and softly walked to the galley. She left them alone.

The silence accentuated the nervous beat of Sapphy's heart, and she rubbed her ears to quiet it. It was difficult to appear calm when her whole world was falling apart. Dante had responded to her on a physical level, and she had believed that they had chance at a real marriage. Finding the divorce papers signed and waiting for her signature had shattered her hopes. She didn't want to walk away, but she wasn't about to beg him to keep her.

"Cosmo will meet us at the airport," he said. "He's compiled a report on your new-found family."

"I didn't ask for you to contact him. He knew I was coming. There is also no reason for me to rely on a bunch of strangers' confirmations about my family when I am more than able to see to it myself."

A tiny prickle of annoyance ran down her spine. Even her friend was conspiring with Dante. Couldn't these overbearing brutes leave her alone?

"You don't need to act on my behalf any longer. I'm capable of handling my affairs," she added.

Dante ran his palm down his face, rubbing his chin as his Adam's apple bobbed. His eyes darkened and his gaze narrowed, but he didn't speak. Turning on his heels, he walked to the private quarters shaking his head.

The silence stung more than a reprimand, much more than a fight could have. At least he would have told her why he was angry.

Determined not to let his display of temper pass with no explanation, she jumped to her feet and stomped into his suite with as much noise as she could make. Sapphy slammed the door and leaned against it. She crossed her arms over her heaving chest, determined to get her answers. Unable to continue with the charade of a happy couple, she confronted her fears.

"What do you want form me, Dante?" She stared at his back as he removed his jacket and placed over a chair. The casual and unaffected attitude speared through her like a sword. "I don't understand. You're getting everything you want without any objection. You have no right to be pissy at me."

He turned and glared at her. "Pissy?"

"Yes. Rude. Nasty. Annoyed." Her nails dug into her palm, but she kept her fist clenched. Her heart hammered in her chest and she forced herself to exhale. "And unpredictable."

"In that case, *bambolina*, it is you who is pissy." Dante threw his tie over the jacket and unbuttoned his shirt. "You are the one who decided to leave the country and told your husband nothing about it. How does that look?"

"I don't care how it looks anymore." The blood rushed to her head and her cheeks flushed with heat. "Stop pretending, Dante. I admit it. I'm not strong enough, not mature enough, and no longer willing to play this game. I signed your stupid papers and had them filed at the courthouse. You will be a free man in a matter of weeks and will never need to care how I make you look ever again."

He stopped in the middle of unbuckling his belt and stared at her. His gaze, questioning and confused, searched her face for what seemed like hours.

"What papers?"

"The divorce papers," she spat, swiping at the damn tears she couldn't control. Her voice cracked, but she willed herself to finish before she broke in to sobs. "You no longer have any responsibilities to the *bambolina*. We are business partners and nothing more. There is no proper way to appear to the public. You are a single man, entitled to live his life. You are free."

Slowly, and with tender movements, he came to her. Raising his hand, he cupped her face and brushed his thumb over her wet cheek.

"And what if I don't want to be free?" he asked in a low voice, laced with deep emotion. "What if I want the responsibility of my *bambolina*?" Lowering his head, he pressed his nose against her cheek and lingered there, pulling her against him and encapsulating her in his arms. "What if I won't let you go?"

No matter what she did, or how hard she tried, Sapphy couldn't resist him. *One last time.* She'd allow herself to be with him just one more time. She needed this act of physical love for closure.

"*Caro*, hold me." Dropping her body against his, she buried her face in his chest and reveled in the strength of his arms and the comfort of his masculine scent. The fresh, clean, and sturdy haze wrapped around her and heartened her confidence as a woman.

She was damned to live an unfulfilled life. He completed her, and she would need to let him go.

Dante's hands splayed across her back, his fingertips composing a melody of possession on her skin as they travelled over her body and ignited a fire she'd tried to extinguish in the previous torturous hours. Searing her neck with kisses, he breathed passion into her being and revitalized her tired psyche with each stroke of his tongue.

"You are my wife, Sapphyra. I *will* care for you, regardless if you want to deny me."

Refusing to hear him, she closed her eyes and allowed herself only to feel. For the moment, Dante was her complete world. There was nothing but their hearts beating in unison, their bodies melding as one, and the loss of her soul to a man who would inevitably leave her. But she was an addict, and he was her drug. Dante was all she craved and desired. She could not, would not, deprive herself of his touch.

"I don't deny you," she breathed. "I'm here."

Peeling the clothes from her body, he tossed them across the sterile chamber. The fervor in his touch commandeered the energy enabling her legs to hold her and her knees buckled. Catching her in his embrace, his lips never leaving her skin, he carried her to the bed and placed her on the white comforter with only her panties and bra to cover her.

"I, and only I, will have you." His dark gaze held the intensity of a man fighting for survival.

For an unknown reason, she nodded.

"You cannot change your mind and walk away from me after this," he breathed.

She shook her head. Placing her feet on the mattress, she bent her legs and raised her hips to remove her panties, but his hands covered hers and stilled her actions. A grin spread across his face as he raised his brows.

"I'd like the privilege," he said, weaving his fingers beneath the lace. "It is like unwrapping a Christmas present I've been waiting for all year long. Only, I've waited for you much longer. This is it Sapphyra. You know what this means, and there is no hesitation any longer. This is the turning point."

She knew. She knew this was a final act. This was goodbye.

The lace teased the side of her thighs, as Dante lowered the pretty garment with care. Then, a groan escaped from deep in his throat like a growl from a starved wolf. "To hell with saving the wrapping paper. I want the gift."

One palm covered her belly, his other hand freed her breasts, and then his mouth captured her straining nipple, teasing it between his lips with the utmost of urgency. It was as if he needed her taste to exist. His teeth scraped over the aching peak as his mouth moved between the valley of her chest to the other. Her skin tingled with excitement. Her breath labored with anticipation.

Accepting his mark on her body, she arched her back and offered him more. Tangling her fingers in his hair, she pulled his face to hers and met his lips. Instantly devoured by the potency of their passion, her love for Dante validated her craving to be with him under any circumstance.

Dampness pooled between her thighs, and her core pulsed with need for him. Nudging her legs further apart, he settled his chest against her, and she felt his heartbeat vibrate through her body. She reached for his thick length and caressed the hot, velvet tip, moist with his desire. She wanted him like nothing before in her life.

Guiding him to her entrance, her hand trembled as she met his gaze. She moaned as he cupped the flesh of her bottom and lifted her to meet him. Then in a single, determined thrust, he was inside her, stretching and filling her essence with pure pleasure. Her fingers grasped his shoulders, and she closed her eyes, climbing the throngs of ecstasy with each euphoric drive of his hips.

"Open your eyes," he demanded. "I want to see those beautiful eyes glazed over with longing for me." He pushed deeper, filling her completely and bringing her that much closer to the edge of wanton abandon. "I want you to see what you do to me."

There was buzzing in her ears as tingles shot from her toes to her core. She let out her breath and her orgasm exploded. Shattering her last sense of control, the light splintered to thousands of pieces. She bucked her hips and pulled him into the erotic abyss of their lovemaking.

Dante threw back his head and released himself deep inside her with a loud sound of unbridled passion.

"*Ti amo, Sapphyra. Sempre, ti amo,*" he breathed, settling against the crook of her neck and placing tiny kisses on the sensitive skin.

His words rang in her mind and tears streamed from her eyes. It wasn't enough. It wasn't right. It was too late. She moved beneath him and turned her face toward the door. No need for him to see her cry.

A buzzing sounded, and she looked over her shoulder to see Dante reach for an intercom button. "Not now!" he snapped.

"*Tesoro*, what is wrong?"

She bit her lip and shook her head, turning away again.

"No," he said, guiding her chin back to him. "You can't call my name in the throw of passion when we make love, and then cry in misery without telling me why."

Her hands flew to her face, disgusted with her lack of composure. He had said all the right things, made her feel like a woman atop of the world, and the only thing she could think of was her future without him. Why couldn't she stay in the moment? Why couldn't she enjoy what she had for now?

Worry crossed his handsome features and his sensuous mouth distorted in a twist as his eyes clouded.

"Is there..." he hesitated and looked away. With his eyes lowered to their clasped hands, he rubbed the back of her palm and scraped his teeth over his lower lip. "Do you regret being with me because there is someone else?"

Never before had she seen him insecure. Never had she imagined that he would doubt her. She wanted no one but Dante Morelli by her side, but if letting him go meant easing his concern, she would do it.

"Not for me, *amore*." Sapphy reached for his face and caressed his sculpted jaw. "I'm sorry if I made you uncomfortable, but I'm not crying any longer. It's difficult to keep things straight, and I think that I confused the two aspects our relationship."

A perplexed expression replaced the worry on his face, and she rushed to clarify her previous statement. "Don't worry. I've signed the papers—"

"The papers," he exclaimed, getting to his feet and walking to the corner table holding a laptop. "Who did you give them to? I need to stop him."

"Stop him?" Damn, she was being emotional, too hormonal for her own good.

"Yes, from filing them," he replied, turning the computer on. "It will be much more difficult to retract them once they have been legally received."

Retract them? The tears returned as the realization of his words hit her. He didn't want the divorce!

"You didn't want the papers filed?"

"Me?" His hand cut the air in front of him. "No."

"Then why did you leave them on the desk for me to sign?"

"I did not leave them for you to sign," he assured her. "The divorce petition has been on my desk for months. I refused to present it to you because I was hoping you'd change your mind, and we could tear it up and continue with our life together."

Stunned by his admission, she pinched the inside her wrist to be sure she wasn't dreaming.

"*Tesoro mio*," he drawled, returning to her side. "I know that I was not your choice of husband. It was thrust upon you when you were only beginning to live as a woman."

"Thrust upon me?"

He held up his hand, asking her not to interrupt. "I was not exactly husband material. I was inexperienced and immature. I did not want to embarrass you."

"You could never embarrass me."

"Please, don't mollify me. I was there, I know the truth." He lowered his head. "You had just begun your education. You were seeing the world outside of your father's house for the first time, and I had no right to rein you in to my house without your consent."

Sapphy stared at the man now kneeling naked at her side. She combed his hair back from his forehead with her fingers, not believing what he was saying.

"You gave up your life for me," she whispered. "You didn't want me for your wife."

"No." He raised his brows, negating her statement. "I only wanted you for my wife. I have always loved you, *bella*. The summer we spent windsurfing and on the water, I knew that one day I would have to win your heart."

"You had my heart," she breathed.

"You were still a child. It was not right to act on my feelings. I battled with myself not to influence your choices and to stay away from you physically. I was selfish, but I knew right from wrong. When we were married, I was relieved." He looked away, bringing her hand to his lips and kissing it.

The tenderness and love permeated her skin, and she accepted it whole-heartedly. She was overjoyed, but she couldn't understand why he hadn't told her how he felt all this time. It would have changed everything, would have made life much simpler.

"Again, selfish of me, but I was glad that you agreed to the wedding." He held her hand to her chest.

"You see, even if our vows were a business agreement, I knew you well enough to know that you would take them seriously and would not turn to another man."

"I didn't." She held his hand tight and pulled it toward her heart. He wanted her for himself.

"But, I knew that with the loss of your father and with my father's illness, I had to learn to provide for us and to preserve our company. I was young and inexperienced. The economy was changing, and the company was barely surviving. The company needed to be revamped, and I had to prove myself worthy of you and your trust."

Sapphy twisted her earring. "I didn't know."

"Know what?"

"That you wanted me. That you loved me."

"I've always loved you. I *love* you."

Dante laughed, his gaze sparkling, as he brought his mouth to hers and kissed her. Tasting the warmth and honesty on his lips, her stomach did a victory somersault, and she repeated her silent prayer, thanking God for Dante.

"I love you, too," she said, placing her hands on the sides of his face and resting her forehead against his.

"I know," he replied, pulling her into his arms and breathing against her hair. "Who did you give the papers to, *bambolina*?"

Her heart skipped a beat. She swallowed and tried to subdue the panic rising in her throat.

"I know it wasn't Antonio," he continued, apparently not alarmed. "He would have told me."

"No. I filed them myself."

His eyes grew big in disbelief. "Why? Why were you in such a hurry to make the divorce official?"

"I wasn't." She intertwined her fingers and twisted

her arms. "I think I was in shock. I was too embarrassed to trust anyone with what was happening."

He paced the room for a few minutes, pinching the bridge of his nose as he did when he was nervous. Then, he typed something on the laptop and came back to her when he had sent it.

"Antonio will take care of the officials in the morning," he said. "He will pull the papers and make the trail disappear." Caressing the top of her head, he grinned. "The worst thing that will happen is that you will marry me again.

She rose to her knees and grasped his hands. "Actually, I'd like that. I've always wanted a big wedding on the estate in Zakynthos. I can wear a full white train, and you can wear a tuxedo. Just like it's supposed to be." She closed her eyes and pictured them reciting their vows atop the cliff with the white-capped waves rolling into the little alcove below them. As the breeze picked up her veil, he'd lean forward and kiss her.

"A big wedding in Greece will make you happy?"

She nodded.

"What are you doing next Sunday?" Dante asked.

"Marrying you," she replied wistfully.

Capturing her lips, he guided her back to the mattress, placing kisses up and down her throat. "Tell me," he said, bracing himself on his elbows. "Do you want to do this before or after you deed your aunt the house?"

"Any sister of my father would not mind if I used her house as a honeymoon escape." She wrapped her arms under his and crossed them behind his back. Licking her lips, she smiled. "Are you going to kiss me again?"

Chapter Twelve

Showered and dressed, Dante and Sapphy made their way through immigration and customs to the international arrivals area at John F. Kennedy Airport. As the doors slid open, Sapphy caught a glimpse of Cosmo waiting for them. He was surrounded by people with huge bouquets of flowers in their arms.

"Was that Petos?" Dante asked.

"Where?"

"Next to Cosmo," he replied pulling their cases behind him.

The next time the door slid open, they walked through and Cosmo shrugged his shoulders as a petite gray haired woman with piercing blue eyes opened her arms for Sapphy.

"I would know you anywhere, my child," the older woman said, wrapping Sapphy in her embrace and dangling roses against her back. "You are Andrea's daughter. I know that with every ounce of air I breathe."

"Thea Eleni?" Sapphy breathed.

"*Ne, paidi mou*. It is me." Tears filled Thea Eleni's eyes as she kissed Sapphy. "You have our eyes, my mother's beautiful hair, and I would not miss you in a crowd of a million people." She pulled on Sapphy's neck and crushed her against her chest. "I never believed my memories were a figment of my imagination. I knew they were real. I've waited and prayed for years about this."

Engulfed by other family members holding flowers, Sapphy looked up to the grinning face Andreas Petos. "Welcome, Sapphyra," he said, much like the patriarch of the family. "Let me make some introductions."

Thea Eleni held up her hand and touched Dante's arm. "And you, young man, I owe your family my gratitude. It was your father who caught me in his arms and your father who saved my brother's life." She held his hands and rose on her toes to kiss his cheek. "You are also the man who has been by my niece's side since my brother passed away. I thank you from the deepest part of my heart."

Andreas draped his arm across Sapphy's shoulder and whispered against her ear. "I'm so happy you came."

She flashed him a smile and wrapped her arm around his waist, giving him a quick squeeze. "Me, too."

"And don't worry, I've collected her DNA sample without letting her know so that you can be sure, and she won't be insulted," he said in a low voice. "I'll give it to Cosmo for the lab."

Sapphy didn't ask for it, she didn't want it. She had all the proof she needed right before her. "We'll talk later."

"So, are you hungry?" Thea Eleni asked Dante. "I've prepared a little meal and some *spanakopita* for tonight. We're all set for dinner, but if you're tired, I'll understand."

Sapphy checked her watch. It was well past dinnertime, but the spinach pie sounded very tempting. Her stomach made a gleeful gurgle.

"*Spanakopita* is Sapphy's favorite," Dante informed her aunt and then turned to Andreas. "Are we far?"

"No. Grandmother's house is in Queens," Andreas said, still hugging Sapphy against his side. "It's only about fifteen minutes away."

"Good." Dante glanced at the remainder of the family and nodded. "We would love dinner. It will allow us the opportunity to invite you all to our wedding."

"But you're already married," said a teenage girl with the same blue eyes as Sapphy's.

"We are," Dante confirmed. "But we'd like to have a party where the whole family could celebrate our love with us."

"That will be wonderful," Thea Eleni said, dabbing the corner of her eyes with a white handkerchief.

"It will be perfect," Sapphy added and winked at her husband. "We would like to do it in Zakynthos, at your home, Thea."

The matriarch wept openly. "I wasn't sure if the house was habitable any longer."

Dante nodded that was the case.

"I never imagined that I'd get to return, but going back with my brother's daughter is more than I could have ever asked for. Thank you, *agape mou*."

Sapphy felt like she was floating on a silver-lined cloud. She'd accomplished what her father had asked, and she would turn the land over to her aunt when Cosmo gave her the paperwork. SD Holdings was safe and flourishing. Most importantly, she was with the man she loved, and the man who loved her.

Exiting the terminal, she weaved her hand

through Dante's arm and looked up at him. *"Ti amo, caro."*

"Sempre, bambolina. Ti amo, sempre."

About the Author

Born in Athens, Greece and raised in the states, Aleka has straddled the Atlantic and had a foot on each continent for many years. An avid reader from a very young age, she entered her first literary contest at twelve with a poem in her native Greek language. The poem placed second in the international competition and ricocheted Aleka's love for writing to the top of her list.

High school and college proved to be a battle between journalism and graduation. However, the need to finish her degrees kept her writing private until her desire to write was no longer containable, and she ended her management career to write fulltime. Aleka's efforts paid off, and her initial publishing contract was a present delivered on time for Christmas. Her novella, Sempre, was published in the Holiday in the Heart Romance Anthology.

Today, Aleka spends her days with her family enjoying the simple pleasures in life. She loves to travel and does so with every excuse available to her. Blending her life passions of storytelling, travel, and exotic cultures, Aleka aims to transport her readers into the magical world of romance.

Thank You!

We appreciate your purchase of this Resplendence Publishing title. We hope your reading experience was a pleasurable one, and invite you to take 10% off your next electronic book purchase from website.

Visit www.ResplendencePublishing.com, select any title, and enter the following code when you check out: **ReadRP10**. This code is valid only on our website, for electronic book purchases only.

During your visit to www.ResplendencePublishing.com, you can enjoy Free Reads from RP's hottest authors, obtain information on our Read Green charitable donation program, or sign up for our quarterly newsletter and our RP Reader Rewards program, which awards loyal readers with a $10.00 gift certificate for every $100.00 spent.

You can also join us on MySpace, Facebook, and Blogspot. You will find regular updates, information on upcoming releases and appearances, as well as contests for free RP titles. We love to hear from our readers, and hope to see you there.

Thank you again for your purchase, and we look forward to becoming your number one resource for high quality electronic fiction.

Best,
The RP Team

Also Available from Resplendence Publishing

The Greek Rule by Aleka Nakis

Ambitious and beautiful Athena Lakis has one simple rule... *No romance with a Greek.*

In theory, this tenet should be easy to keep. After all, reaching for her lifelong dream to own and operate a prestigious hotel on prime seaside property in Greece, she has her hands full. The major hurdle being her drop-dead gorgeous competition: Greek tycoon Alexandros Strintzaris.

Alexandros has his sights set on more than just a real estate deal. He wants Athena, and he always gets what he wants. When he discovers she is the one outbidding him on the resort, will he feel the same?

From a Naples ballroom to the exotic island of Santorini, Alexandros and Athena learn when it comes to affairs of the heart, there are always exceptions to the rule.

The Summer Deal by Aleka Nakis

Samantha Mallone is a smart, beautiful redhead who is oblivious of the magnetic affect she has on her charismatic boss.

International billionaires don't lie to get a woman, but Demosthenis Lakis does just that to lure his assistant to Greece.

Unaware of her employer's true motivations, Samantha eagerly prepares for a summer in the Mediterranean when her psychotic-ex calls and threatens her, prompting Mr. Lakis to arrange for her to leave New York immediately.

Abroad, Mr. Lakis changes the ground rules: they're in Greece where formalities are foreign. Samantha becomes Sammy, and Mr. Lakis becomes Demo. Sexual tension burns as the big-eyed Sammy tours the ancient ruins on Demo's arm and discovers his intent to show her there is more to their relationship than business.

Proving to be unlike other men from Sammy's past, Demo puts their passionate summer deal to the test of a lifetime...

Eyes of the Dead by Aleka Nakis

What would you endure to find the cure for the disease that killed your mother? Exposure to venomous snakes? Raging rapids without a life jacket? Drug lords who dab in sex trafficking?

Would you relinquish control and trust your life in a dead man's hands?

Tiffany Jensen, a young breast cancer researcher, confronts her greatest fear and flies on a plane to a foreign country alone. Venturing into the dangerous terrain of the Mayan jungle, she is willing to do just about anything for the cure.

Antonio Francisco Fernandez, aka Agent AFFCROC, is open to only one possibility: getting Tiffany out of his territory and safely back to the States. Will his insistence deny her success, or struggling to find her way, will she come face to face with the eyes of the dead?

Le PACS by Tatiana March

Stephanie Forssell accepts a weekend on a yacht in Cannes, unaware that she is expected to sleep with any man on board. When a rugged Texan demands his rights, she chooses to jump in the sea rather than comply.

Grant Buchanan hates hookers. They remind him of his faithless mother. The slim blonde tempts him, and when he learns his mistake, he can't get her out of his mind.

He tracks Stephanie down and makes her an offer. She agrees to spend three months with him, on the condition that they contract "Le PACS" —the French civil partnership intended for gay couples but now a fashionable alternative to marriage.

Grant is determined to prove Stephanie worthless. Stephanie believes she is sacrificing herself to raise money for a noble cause.

Neither is prepared to make any concessions, but as the weeks go by, the battle of wills turns into a campaign for love.

Dictated by Fate by Fran Lee

Chris has been through hell, is about to be homeless, and her situation is showing no signs of improvement. She knows there is no such thing as a knight in shining armor—she learned that the hard way. Now she's on the brink of total disaster with no champion to save her.

Tonio is being shoved toward an unwelcome, unwanted marriage, and is quickly running out of options. It boils down to a choice between getting hogtied to a woman he can't stand, or quickly finding an attractive substitute who can be the band-aid he needs without becoming a full-body cast.

When Chris and Tonio meet, fate intervenes with a vengeance. They each make assumptions about the other's lifestyle choices, and assume that a no-strings attached relationship between them is the perfect solution. But you know what they say happens when you assume...

Beauty and the Feast by Julia Barrett

Eva Raines is an uncomplicated country girl who's all about food. Eva moves to the Napa Valley where her culinary skills come to the attention of the owners of a start-up, *All Things to All People*, and Eva finds her niche as a personal chef. Now all she needs is a man as perfect as her cooking, but she has serious doubts that such a creature exists.

When wealthy entrepreneur, winery owner, and noted lothario, Gabriel Abbott, makes plans to seduce his flavor of the month, his assistant hires *All Things to All People* to cater a gourmet dinner. Eva expects to use her way with food to showcase the startup. What she unexpectedly discovers is that her culinary skills showcase far more.

Once Gabriel finds himself seduced by Eva's voice, and the sensual flavors and textures of her food, his previous plans are quickly forgotten. He begins to obsess about meeting his little chef in person. But when Eva and Gabe finally come face to face, the question is, how hot will their fire burn?

New York Fairytale by Elaine Lowe

Ronnie Carmichael will never be compared to Snow White, Sleeping Beauty or the frickin' Little Mermaid. She is forty, with a ten-year-old kid, an annoying ex-husband, a fledging business and a night job as a bartender. She knows there is no such thing as Prince Charming, no Mr. Right. But she'd be more than happy to have the hot guy in the tuxedo sitting at her bar as her Mr. Right Now.

When Rudy Vidmar walked into the little tapas restaurant, looking to escape the weight of a country's needs that constantly rest on his shoulders, he didn't expect to be completely charmed by the saucy New Yorker behind the bar. She is sexy and wild and exactly what he needs. A satisfying romp in a walk-in freezer, though hot enough to melt ice, just isn't enough. He wants more.

But what will Ronnie think when she finds out that 'Rudy' is actually Prince Giorgio Rudolpho Frederick Von Lieberstein Vidmar, ruler of the tiny, troubled principality of Marvinia? Will she continue to question Fate, or will she accept their encounter as the beginning of her very own New York Fairytale?

Find Resplendence titles at the following retailers

Resplendence Publishing
www.ResplendencePublishing.com

Amazon
www.Amazon.com

Barnes and Noble
www.BarnesandNoble.com

Target
www.Target.com

Fictionwise
www.Fictionwise.com

All Romance E-Books
www.AllRomanceEBooks.com

Mobipocket
www.Mobipocket.com

1 Place for Romance
www.1PlaceForRomance.com

Printed in Great Britain
by Amazon